'Jo will loo
heard Angel
had taken a s

Jo turned to fac , her arms linked
defensively across her midriff. She blinked,
and something shifted inside her as she took
in the tender picture of Brady and his infant
son.

He held him close, tucked into the crook of
his arm, one large, masculine hand cradling
his son's tiny feet. And they looked so right
together. Already a family. Jo felt a wash of
emotion she couldn't explain.

'Jo.' Brady's mouth made a brief twist of
acknowledgment.

'Hello, Brady.'

BACHELOR DADS
Single Doctor…Single Father!

At work they are skilled medical professionals, but at home, as soon as they walk in the door, these eligible bachelors are on full-time fatherhood duty!

These devoted dads still find room in their lives for love…

It takes very special women to win the hearts of these dedicated doctors, and a very special kind of caring to make these single fathers full-time husbands!

A MOTHER
FOR HIS BABY

BY
LEAH MARTYN

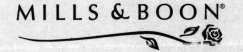

MILLS & BOON®

First published in Great Britain 2006
Harlequin Mills & Boon Limited,
Eton House, 18-24 Paradise Road, Richmond, Surrey TW9 1SR

© Leah Martyn 2006

ISBN-13: 978 0 263 84775 8
ISBN-10:   0 263 84775 6

Set in Times Roman 10½ on 12¾ pt
03-1206-47599

Printed and bound in Spain
by Litografia Rosés, S.A., Barcelona

Leah Martyn loves to create warm, believable characters for the Medical Romance™ series. She is grounded firmly in rural Australia, and the special qualities of the bush are reflected in her stories. For plots and possibilities, she bounces ideas off her husband on their early-morning walks. Browsing in bookshops and buying an armful of new releases is high on her list of enjoyable things to do.

Recent titles by the same author:

DR CHRISTIE'S BRIDE
THE BUSH DOCTOR'S RESCUE
CHRISTMAS IN THE OUTBACK
THE DOCTOR'S MARRIAGE

For Marina

CHAPTER ONE

'I FORGOT to ask.' Jo stopped abruptly and caught Fliss's arm. 'Who's the best man?'

'Brady McNeal. Friend of the groom. He's a doctor.'

'At least half the wedding guests are,' Jo said with pithy humour. 'Is he local?'

'McNeal? Don't think so. Someone said he's just arrived back from overseas. If you'd been at Sophie's hen party you'd have heard all about him.'

'Well, if I hadn't been on holidays I would have been there.'

'Our little gang of three is breaking up, isn't it?' Fliss sounded a note of regret. 'Seems only last week when we graduated. And now Soph and Ben are relocating to Sydney, you're stuck in your rural practice at Mt Pryde and I'm the only one left here.'

'Hey, you, don't get maudlin.' Jo gave Fliss's shoulder a little squeeze. 'We'll have to organise a regular get-together or something.'

Fliss's face lit up. 'We could do that, couldn't we? Either in Sydney or here in Brisbane.'

'Or you could both come to me.'

Fliss rolled her eyes.

'For heaven's sake!' Jo remonstrated laughingly. 'Mt Pryde is barely a two-hour drive from the city'.

'Honey, two *minutes* from the city and I get withdrawal symptoms. The sticks aren't for me. But I know you love it there,' Fliss placated her friend quickly. 'I just don't know what on earth you find to *do*. And how could you possibly meet any men!'

Jo shook her head, giving the silk wrap over her bare shoulders a little straightening twitch. They'd been down this road a dozen times. Fliss loved the buzz of working in a state-of-the-art city clinic where they specialised in sports medicine, while she herself relished the grass-roots nature of medicine in a country practice where everyone knew the doctors and the doctors knew one another's patients almost as well as their own families.

'Oh, look!' Fliss gave a muted squeal. 'Here's the bride now. Oh, bless… Doesn't she look gorgeous?'

'Yes.' Jo's reply was soft but heartfelt as she watched Sophie, on the arm of her father, moving slowly towards them along the paved walkway for her wedding to her soul-mate, Ben Landers.

Would she ever be so lucky? Jo wondered. At thirty-two she'd had several relationships but they hadn't lasted and she certainly hadn't met a man she'd wanted to spend the rest of her life with, laugh with, have babies with. But Sophie and Ben had it all.

'Let's get a bit closer.' Fliss hooked her arm through Jo's and manoeuvred them to within smiling distance of the groom and his best man, who were standing with the marriage celebrant against the backdrop of rainforest in the Brisbane botanic gardens.

Seeing them, Ben grinned and mock-swiped his brow in a *thank heavens she's here* kind of gesture.

'As *if*,' Fliss mouthed, and made a small face back at the bridegroom.

Jo caught none of the interplay between the two. Her eyes were riveted on the best man. Brady McNeal was all male. Impressive height with broad shoulders delineated by the superbly cut charcoal suit. And not bad-looking either.

There was a moment when he turned his dark head towards Jo and smiled. A smile that was wry, slightly lopsided, and was gone in a blink.

The fact that it sent slivers of warmth to every corner of her body was immaterial. Jo dipped her head, convinced her cheeks were on fire and thanking heaven no one had noticed. Instead, all eyes were on the bride as she took her place beside her groom and slipped her hand into his.

'Wasn't it a lovely ceremony?' Fliss sighed. 'I think I'd like something just like that.'

'Someone in mind?' Jo said jokingly, as they trotted along on their higher than high heels up the street towards the restaurant where the reception was to be held.

'Mind your own, Josephine.'

'So there is!' Jo dug her friend in the ribs. 'You drama queen. Who is he?'

'Daniel,' Fliss said airily. 'He's a pilot.'

'Well that makes a change. Why isn't he with you?'

'He's overnighting to Perth or he would have been.'

'Oh, well, that just leaves me unattached,' Jo said philosophically.

Fliss sent her an arch look. 'Plenty of eye candy amongst the guest list, babe. What about Brady McNeal?'

Jo felt heat scorch her cheeks. 'Don't be daft.'

'According to the goss, he's single.' Fliss waggled well-shaped brows suggestively.

'And I'll be miles away from here by this time tomorrow,' Jo pointed out in exasperation. 'Get real.'

'She who hesitates...' Fliss trilled.

'Oh, ha,' Jo said in a bored voice. 'Look, here we are.' Grabbing Fliss by the elbow, she steered them off the street into the up-market restaurant.

Brady McNeal looked around him. The reception was in full swing, the hum of conversation filling the small, intimate restaurant. It had been a nice wedding and he'd enjoyed himself more than he'd expected to.

He hadn't really known anyone except Ben. And Sophie he'd met only recently. But they'd managed to sort him out and he'd met most of their friends—except the cool-looking blonde he'd made eye contact with in the gardens.

When Sophie had dragged him over to their table to 'meet the guys' as she'd termed it, the blonde had been at another table, in a huddle with Sophie's parents and with her back to him.

Well, what did it matter anyway? He was miles away from pursuing a new relationship. That possibility had gone out the window months ago. When Tanya had simply walked away from him.

Leaving *him* to pick up the pieces of the life they could have had together.

In his more fanciful moments, Brady likened the hurt she'd left behind to a thorn embedded so deeply it could never be removed. He could only hope that one day enough scar tissue would have formed over the hurt so that he barely felt it any more.

And maybe someday he'd find someone special to share his life with. And maybe not. Oh, hell, it was all too difficult, he thought, pulling back the sleeve of his white shirt to glance at his watch.

His mouth compressed slightly. Another couple of hours should see his official duties here ended and he could decently make his exit.

And next week he would begin a new phase of his life. The small rural town with its ring of blue mountains was calling him. He just hoped and prayed he'd made the right decision.

The newlyweds had left the reception and the farewells were still echoing in Jo's head as she made her way swiftly along the city block to the parking station.

Some of the guests were going on to a nightclub and Fliss had tried to coax her along, but Jo had declined. She had to drive back to Mt Pryde early the next day to be ready for surgery on Monday.

Saturday night revellers spilled out of a pub, jostling each other, and Jo sidestepped quickly out of the way. After only a couple of nights in the city, she was longing for the relative tranquillity of her country lifestyle.

Crossing the street to where the deserted high-rise buildings lent a somewhat eerie feel to the atmosphere, Jo shivered slightly, taking a tighter grip on the strap of her little beaded shoulder-bag. It was then she became aware someone was following closely behind.

She quickened her steps, relieved to see the neon sign of the parking station up ahead. I don't need this, she said silently, increasing her pace until she was almost running.

'Hey!' A deep voice rang out behind her. 'It's OK. I'm from Ben and Sophie's wedding party—Brady McNeal.'

Spinning round Jo put her hand to her heart. 'Oh—it *is* you.'

'Sorry. I didn't mean to frighten you.' Brady's dark gaze homed in on her sudden pallor. 'You OK?'

Jo managed a weak smile, feeling slightly foolish. 'I will be now I know I'm not about to be mugged. We didn't get to meet at the wedding,' she added breathlessly, holding out her hand. 'I'm Jo.'

'Hi.' Brady took her hand. 'You're the third doctor.'

Jo blinked. 'Sorry?'

He grinned. 'Sophie mentioned the gang of three. You, she and Fliss. You all trained together, didn't you?'

'Ah…yes. We've been friends for ages. And you're a friend of Ben's, I take it?'

He nodded. 'We trained together, too.'

Jo gave a little laugh. 'This is all a bit ridiculous, isn't it?'

Brady's smile was slow and a bit lopsided. 'Perhaps we were destined to meet.'

Jo took a small step backwards, clasping the silk of her wrap more tightly across her chest. Was this a chat-up line? 'Are you parked nearby?' she countered awkwardly.

Well, he'd stuffed that up nicely. Brady had seen the sudden defensiveness hazing her green eyes. 'I'm collecting my car from the parking station,' he said briskly. 'I imagine you're on the same errand?'

'Yes.' Jo licked her lips, her heart thumping and pattering. They began walking again. 'Are you just in town for the wedding?' she asked conversationally.

'My movements are a bit fluid at the moment.'

Well, that seemed to be that. Jo scrabbled in her purse

for her parking receipt. 'I'm on the third floor,' she said, assuming they would say their goodbyes.

'Me, too.' Brady summoned the lift and waited for her to get in.

In the few seconds while the lift groaned its way upwards, the silence was awkward. Keeping her gaze carefully averted, Jo took a sneaky look at Brady McNeal as he hooked his suit jacket over his shoulder and slouched against the opposite wall of the lift. Nice eyes, she thought, and cheekbones to die for, and the snug fit of his suit trousers indicated a pair of long, muscular legs. She was still fanatisising when the lift jerked to a stop.

'I'll walk with you to your car.' He took her elbow firmly as they vacated the lift. 'These places are spooky at the best of times.'

And she was parked at the very end of a long, long row of vehicles. 'Perhaps we should have both taken cabs in the first place,' she suggested on a laugh made brittle by a flood of nerves when his guiding hand on her elbow slid down to entwine her fingers in his.

It was the lightest contact, casual and probably without meaning, yet Jo was suddenly, vividly aware of Brady's masculinity. For an instant some maverick part of her longed for him to stop and whirl her into his arms. Hold her close. Kiss her…

'Nah.' Brady vetoed the idea of taxis with a huff of amusement. 'I prefer to have my own wheels handy. You can never find a cab when you need one.'

'And there always seem to be twenty people in line before you,' she agreed, in a voice that was too high and too bright. 'It was a nice wedding, wasn't it?' Determined to keep up the innocuous chatter, Jo changed conversation channels quickly.

'Uh, yes, it was. Let's hope they can stay the distance.'

'Of course they will. They're dotty about each other.'

The corners of Brady's mouth tucked in on a small grimace. 'There are valid reasons to go into marriage other than being *dotty* about each other, Jo.'

'Reasons like money or position?' Jo couldn't keep the faint note of censure out of her voice.

Brady was taken aback. They weren't his reasons at all. Would never be. *His* reasons were entirely personal. Way too personal to share with someone he'd just met. Even someone as delectable as the lady by his side. A slow, fence-mending smile edged his mouth. 'No. Speaking personally, I'd never want to marry someone for those reasons.'

It was said with obvious sincerity and Jo felt her heart warm again. She managed a fleeting smile. 'I wouldn't either. Ah…' She pointed ahead. 'That's my car at the end, the white hatchback.'

Brady looked at the gleaming paintwork and grinned. 'Been through the carwash for the occasion, has it?'

'Something like that. But by this time tomorrow it's bound to be nice and dusty again,' she predicted ruefully.

Brady's dark brows peaked. 'You don't work here in the city, then?'

'Haven't for ages. I love my relatively quiet existence in a country practice. What about you?'

Brady released her hand abruptly as they came to a halt beside her car. 'For the moment I'm staying with my parents at Bardon. Taking off to a new job shortly.'

'Well, good luck, then.' Hurriedly, Jo delved into her bag again for her keys. Unlocking the door of the car, she stood back for a second. 'It was…nice meeting you, Brady,' she said, a bit stiltedly.

'You, too.' He stretched in front of her to open the door of the car. His shoulder nudged her arm and the side of her breast before she could step out of the way.

'Thanks.' Jo's thoughts were in wild disarray as she slid into the driver's seat. Suddenly, everything that was male about Brady had assailed her. Everything from the clean crisp smell of apple-scented laundry softener on his shirt to the subtle male aftershave on his jaw as he'd swooped across her to open the door. 'Take care, then,' she said from behind the safe haven of her wound-down window.

'And you.' Brady sketched a casual salute, before turning away.

Jo watched as Brady loped back along the row of parked cars and then dodged through the line, obviously to collect his own vehicle.

What was it all about? She gnawed her lip thoughtfully. Perhaps they'd meet up again one day. After all, they had friends in common. The thought wasn't too far-fetched. Jo shivered involuntarily and admitted she would have liked the chance to get to know Brady McNeal better. A whole lot better.

He should have asked for her phone number. Brady started the engine of his car and shot towards the exit sign. He huffed a self-deprecating laugh. Hell, he didn't even know her surname. But Sophie would. His heart somersaulted.

Was he ready for even the most tenuous kind of relationship, though? But in terms of area, Queensland was a vast state. For all he knew, Jo's country practice could be at the opposite end of the state from where he was going. But they could always email. Relationships had been sustained by much less personal contact. His hopes rose briefly and then flagged. Best forget it. Forget Jo with the tiny freckles across her nose and the very sweet way she smiled.

Get real, he admonished himself silently. What woman in her right mind would want you and your baggage, McNeal?

The morning at Mt Pryde Medical Centre began to unfold like a typical Monday. Even before Jo had time to stow her case and switch on her computer, Angelo Kouras, one of the partners, poked his head in.

'Welcome back, stranger. Nice holiday?'

'The best.' Jo's parents ran a bed and breakfast in North Queensland and it was her idea of the perfect holiday; with her mother's fabulous cooking, her dad's extensive wine cellar and nothing to do but swim and snorkel, day in and day out.

'Good trip back?'

'No dramas. What about here?'

'A few, but we handled them.' Angelo tilted a wry smile. 'Ah, staff meeting at one o'clock, Jo. I've asked Monica to cater lunch. We've serious business to discuss.'

Jo frowned. Was a patient about to sue? Or were they simply running out of funding? 'What's up?'

Angelo came in and closed the door. 'Ralph's decided to retire.'

'What—just like that?'

'Said he's been thinking about it for a while. And Lilian's keen to relocate to Brisbane to be near the grand-children apparently.'

Jo's mind began racing. She hated these kinds of changes. They'd have to advertise for a new partner, cull the applicants, make a short-list, interview… She clicked her tongue. 'I've only been out of the place for a month and all this happens.'

Angelo parked himself on the corner of her desk. 'Ralph dropped his bombshell on Tom and me the day after you'd left on holidays. So at least we've had a bit of time to get cracking. Got some ads in *pronto*.'

'Any luck?'

'Six replies. We knocked it down to a short-list of three and selected someone. Sorry, you weren't here for the interviews but I think you'll be happy with our choice. He's been working in rural medicine in Canada for the past couple of years. Seemed to latch on pretty quickly to what we wanted here. And he wants to put down roots.' Angelo grinned. 'And the best part is he's had experience in anaesthetics, which will no doubt please Pen.'

Jo nodded. Angelo's wife, Penny, was the sole fully qualified anaesthetist at the local hospital and was constantly on call. Still, Jo felt slightly miffed that they'd gone ahead and made the selection without her. Her chin came up in query. 'Does this paragon have a name?'

'Brady McNeal. He trained at the Prince Alfred in Melbourne. Excellent CV.'

Jo felt the wind knocked out of her, dropping into her chair as though her strings had been cut. 'Brady McNeal's coming to work here?'

Angelo's dark eyes blinked a bit behind his steel-framed spectacles. 'Well…yes. Is there a problem?'

Make it a thousand. Jo's thoughts were spinning. 'It's just odd, that's all.' She gave a jagged laugh. 'I actually met Dr McNeal at my friend's wedding on Saturday. He was the best man.'

'You're kidding!' Angelo's head rocked back in disbelief 'And he didn't mention his appointment to Mt Pryde at all?'

Jo made a gesture with the palm of her hand. 'I spoke

to him only briefly after the wedding. We'd left our cars at the same parking station and walked along together.'

'Odd he didn't make the connection, though. I mean, he was made aware Josephine Rutherford was our female member of the practice.'

Except she'd introduced herself merely as Jo.

'And we certainly made a point of telling him you'd have been at his interview, except you were on leave,' Angelo went on.

Jo switched her gaze from Angelo's puzzled face to her framed medical certificate on the wall behind him. 'I don't think I used my surname.'

'Ah, that would explain it.' Angelo looked relieved.

'So, when is Dr McNeal joining us?'

'Officially next Monday. But he'll be here today to sign a contract with us and I believe he wants to organise a child-minder for his son.' Angelo slid to his feet. 'I know you have an interest in paeds and you're up to date with the child-care facilities in the town, so I told him you'd be the best person to help him with that,' he added ingenuously.

So the man was obviously married. Jo pushed back a sick kind of resentment. He certainly hadn't acted married—giving her all that attention in the car park. Holding her hand, for heaven's sake! Yet she wouldn't have put him down as a sleaze either.

It was puzzling and disappointing. She'd hoped...well, what had she hoped? She felt her throat close and swallowed. 'Is...his wife coming along with him today?'

Angelo's mouth compressed for a second. 'There's no wife, Jo. Brady is a single father. Not unheard of in this day and age—even in Mt Pryde.'

Jo gathered herself, feeling she'd just fallen down a cliff

and now had to scramble back up. 'When am I to have this meeting with him, then?'

'Three o'clock this afternoon. Vicki will reschedule your list as much as possible. Anything else, I'll cover for you, OK?'

Well, it had to be, didn't it? Jo got to her feet and walked Angelo to the door. 'I'd like to, um, glance through Dr McNeal's CV, acquaint myself with his background a bit before we meet, if that's all right?'

'Of course. See Monica. We can have your input, then, at the meeting. The sooner we get things sorted, the better.'

With Angelo gone, Jo sank onto the edge of her desk, aware of the faint trembling in her fingers as she picked up her mail. She couldn't help but wonder what Dr Brady McNeal's reaction would be when they came face to face again.

CHAPTER TWO

ALMOST in a daze, Jo sorted haphazardly through her mail, finding countless brochures from various drug companies and several postcards from friends who were holidaying overseas. Anything connected with her patients would have already been dealt with by one of the other partners.

She consigned the junk mail to the bin and then, resolving to make her first day back as normal as possible, she made her way along the corridor to the staffroom. Vicki, their receptionist, was busily making coffee, humming cheerily to herself, when Jo walked in.

'One of those for me?'

'Oh—hi, Jo! You're back!' Vicki clattered mugs on to the benchtop and spun round. 'How was the Barrier Reef?'

'Fabulous as always. You'll have to treat yourself and go some time.'

Vicki looked coy. 'Actually, I might just do that—and sooner rather than later. Ta-da!' She held out her left hand. 'Jared and I got engaged. Getting married at Easter.'

'Oh, my stars! Congratulations!' Jo admired the three beautiful little diamonds set on their band of white gold and then wrapped Vicki in a hug. 'Are we all invited?'

'Of course, silly.'

'Just everything's happened since I've been away,' Jo grumbled, pouring her coffee and adding a dollop of milk.

'I know…' Vicki said seriously. 'Ralph's leaving. I wonder how the new doctor will fit in?'

Jo shrugged. 'Time will tell, I guess. Thanks for the coffee, Vic.'

'Welcome.'

Jo took herself along to Reception. 'Good morning, Monica,' she said, greeting their practice manager with a smile.

'Jo. Good to have you back.' Monica looked slightly harassed. 'I take it you've heard the news about Ralph?'

Jo nodded. 'Angelo filled me in. I wanted to look over the new doctor's CV before my meeting with him. Do you have it handy?'

Monica picked up some paperwork from the in-tray. 'Yes, I do. Come through. It's good they found a suitable replacement so quickly,' she said, unlocking her cabinet and handing Jo the file. 'The place couldn't function indefinitely with one doctor down. The workload would be difficult to say the least.'

'It certainly would,' Jo agreed. 'Talking about workloads, I'd better check on my patient list.'

Jo's first patient for the day was Nora Burows. The elderly lady had an extremely fair complexion and years of working outdoors on the family farm had resulted in severe sun damage to her face and arms. Nora was listed for an excision of a scaly lesion on the side of her throat.

With the rate of skin cancer in Australia the highest in the world, Jo wasn't about to take any chances. She'd need to send a sample of the damaged skin to the lab. A biopsy would be carried out and hopefully, for her patient's sake, would return a benign result.

But the depletion of the ozone layers around the world was a real concern. Jo guessed in the not-too-distant future medical officers would be seeing a dramatic increase in the incidence of melanomas.

She buzzed through to their practice nurse in the treatment room. 'Marika, has Mrs Burows arrived yet?'

'I have her settled and we're ready to go when you are.'

'Right. I'm on my way.'

Jo pushed back the pale blue curtain and greeted her patient, who was lying on the treatment couch. 'Good morning, Nora. Ready for your op?'

'As I'll ever be, Doctor.' Nora's lashes around her pale blue eyes fluttered briefly.

'Now, you haven't got yourself all worked up, have you? We've been through a few of these together.'

Nora's throat convulsed as she swallowed. 'Doesn't make it any easier, though, Dr Rutherford.'

'I know.' Jo patted her shoulder. 'So, we'll get rid of this nasty little number for you and you can be on your way.'

Jo double-checked her patient's notes. Nora's blood pressure was a touch low but otherwise she enjoyed reasonable health.

'Right, let's get started. Would you drape, please, Marika?'

Gowned and gloved, Jo expertly drew up lignocaine and slowly began infiltrating the skin around the lesion. 'This will pack quite a strong effect, Nora,' she warned. 'You'll feel some numbing around your ear and lower jaw.' While she waited for the local to take effect, Jo became aware of Nora's sudden rapid breathing and felt a tinge of alarm. 'Are you OK under there, Nora?'

'I don't think I am, Doctor. My tummy's all queasy…'

'Marika, get her feet up, please,' Jo directed sharply.

In a second Marika had slid several pillows under Nora's lower legs and begun to sponge her face.

'Your body is reacting to the anaesthetic, Nora,' Jo said gently. 'Did you eat breakfast?'

'Just a cup of tea.'

'Perhaps your blood sugar's a bit low. Just take some deep breaths and try to relax. That's good, sweetheart. There's no hurry. We'll wait until you're feeling OK again.'

Nora was still shaky when the procedure was finished. 'Lie there for a while,' Jo instructed, 'and then Marika will help you sit up. But very slowly, mind. And dangle your legs over the side for a while until you're feeling stronger. Now, is someone with you?'

Nora clasped her thin hands across her chest. 'My daughter's outside in the waiting room.'

'Good. I think we'll get her to come in and sit with you while you recover.' Jo looked keenly down at her patient. She was still pale. 'I'm sorry this one took a bit longer than usual, Nora.' Jo stripped off her gloves. 'It had spread further than I thought.'

Nora moistened dry lips. 'I…will be all right, though, won't I?'

'I'll have the result of the biopsy in a few days.' Jo avoided answering directly. There was no point in alarming her patient unnecessarily. 'And I'll see you in a week to have the stitches out.'

Jo was already running behind time. 'Same old, same old,' she murmured, going out to Reception to call in her next patient.

She worked slowly through her list and by twelve-thirty

she'd begun to wonder how on earth she was going to make the staff meeting on time.

Then the fates looked kindly on her. Vicki popped her head in. 'Toni Morris just cancelled, Jo. Said her little one's feeling much better. Thinks it was just a twenty-four-hour bug. He's had a light meal, kept it down and is looking brighter.'

Jo pushed her chair back and stretched. 'Excellent. Thanks, Vic.'

Vicki departed with a fluttered wave and Jo swung to her feet and walked to the window. Her consulting room was at the rear of the sprawling low-set building and she loved the view. It was the first week of September and spring had come with a burst of colour. Jo noticed even the old mango tree was drooping with blossoms, ensuring a bumper feast of the tropical fruit for the long hot summer ahead.

How I love this place, she thought, her gaze stretching across to the paddocks already knee-deep in summer crops of baby corn, melons and tomatoes. She shook her head. Why did she have the feeling that everything was about to change?

She turned as her phone rang. It was Angelo, straight to the point.

'Had time to look over Brady's CV yet, Jo?'

Jo stole a guilty look at her watch. 'Just about to. I've been flat to the boards.'

'Me, too. See you in a bit, then.'

'Yes.' So much for holidays, she thought dryly, clipping the receiver back on its rest. She was beginning to feel she'd never been away.

Collecting the file Monica had given her, she dropped back into the chair. 'OK, Brady McNeal,' she murmured, 'let's see what you have to offer.'

With the file on the desk in front of her, Jo leaned forward. In a reflex action she shielded her eyes. It felt odd to be reading the man's very personal background information. Odd and strangely intrusive.

Well, there was nothing she could do about it, she rationalised.

And the further she read, the more she realised Brady McNeal seemed a very good choice for their particular needs. Or was her judgment being clouded by the fact she'd already interacted with the man?

And been attracted.

She took a deep breath, feeling the swirl of mixed emotions well up like a balloon inside her chest.

Jo ran a brush through her hair and added a dash of lipstick, before joining the others in the staffroom for their working lunch.

With quiet efficiency, Monica had set out sandwiches and a fruit platter and topped up the coffee-maker in readiness. 'There's hot water in the vacuum jug if anyone wants to make tea,' she said.

'Oh, yes, please, Monica.' Jo got down a mug and broke open a new packet of teabags.

'One for me too, please, Jo, while you're there.'

Jo heard Ralph Mitchell's voice rumble from the doorway, and smiled. 'Coming up. Angelo?'

'Coffee for me, thanks. I'll get it. Anyone seen Tom?'

'Someone taking my name in vain?' Tom Yardley, the fourth doctor in the practice, catapulted in, dumped several files on the table and whooped, 'Jo! Nice to have you back with us, babe.'

Jo made a face at the fair-haired young man and then

grinned. 'Nice to *be* back.' She liked Tom. He was young, only twenty-nine, but already he was shaping up as an excellent GP. He'd been reared in the district and his parents were still teaching at the local high school. He loved being home again but, of course, these days he had his own place.

'I want to thank you all for being so proactive about this situation,' Ralph said quietly, a bit later, as the doctors sat around the table. 'I hadn't mentioned it before because I didn't want to put more pressure on you to find a new partner, but one of our grandsons has been diagnosed with leukaemia.'

There was a hush around the table. Then Jo said softly, 'I'm so sorry, Ralph.'

'That goes for all of us, mate.' Angelo looked shaken.

Tom had reined in his usual hearty manner to convey earnestly, 'If they've managed to zap it early, the prognosis for childhood leukaemia is very positive these days.'

'We're hanging onto that.' Ralph's face worked for a second. 'And Michael is a stoic little chap. Came through his first lot of chemo pretty well. And the staff at the Mater Children's are nothing short of brilliant.'

'So, I imagine you and Lilian will want to get away as soon as possible…' Jo felt a hard lump in her chest and gripped her tea-mug tightly.

Ralph nodded. 'We'd like to be some support for the parents, of course. There are two younger kiddies. And Karen and Steve naturally want to spend as much time at the hospital with Michael as they can.'

'In that case, don't feel you have to stick around to mentor Brady,' Angelo said decisively. 'I'm sure between the lot of us, plus Monica, we can get him up to speed and feeling a part of the practice in no time.'

'Not than we won't miss you greatly, Ralph.' Jo bit the inside of her bottom lip. In reality, she hated the thought of Ralph leaving. He'd been the anchor at the Mt Pryde medical centre for ages. And whether the staff realised it or not, they all in some way depended on his quiet wisdom and the gentle way he handled matters.

The thought of Brady McNeal, with all his unknown quantities, replacing him was suddenly leaving Jo feeling very unsettled.

As if he'd gauged her thoughts, Ralph linked the medical team with his kind blue gaze. 'I'd like to think the Mt Pryde practice will go on providing quality care for its patients and I know you'll all do your utmost to help Brady settle in. I understand you're giving him a hand to find some suitable care for his son, Jo?'

Jo's mouth turned down at the corners. 'Until I know exactly what kind of hours and so on he'll need, I can't really organise anything. But I will ring around this afternoon and at least get a feel for what's available.'

'A family day care mother might be his best shot,' Tom offered.

'Maybe.' Jo took a steadying breath. 'Dr McNeal may have some ideas of his own.' Well, she hoped he would. 'We'll see later this afternoon, when he gets here.'

Angelo's dark brows peaked. 'And having read his CV, Jo, do you have any reservations about Brady's appointment?'

'He seems well rounded,' Jo said carefully. 'Obviously his experience in rural medicine will stand him in good stead here. And if you all think personality-wise he'll fit in…?'

'I had a long chat to him.' Ralph sought to put Jo's un-certainties to rest. 'I think he'll be very co-operative and he wants to make a home here. That should make all the difference to our acceptance of him and he of us—if that makes sense.' The senior doctor sent a wry smile around the table.

'All the sense in the world,' Angelo concurred heartily. 'And now, Ralph, I know the circumstances of your leaving aren't ideal but you can't slope off without a farewell of some kind.'

'There's really no need—' Ralph's mild protest was howled down immediately. 'Well, all right, then. Thank you all very much. I know Lilian will appreciate it.'

'Good, that's settled, then.' Angelo drained his coffee. 'We'll fit in with you and Lilian. When do you think?'

'We should have our packing finalised by the end of next week,' Ralph said.

'Let's say Saturday evening of next week, then? At our place. Pen and I will barbecue. It might be a good chance for Brady to mingle socially as well.'

With her usual care, Jo worked through her patient list after lunch. But as three o'clock approached, she found her heart was all but leapfrogging in her chest.

She was being ridiculous, she berated herself, especially when she recalled that after she'd read Brady's CV, she'd actually considered calling him on his mobile number and sorting out the fact they'd already met.

And then she'd reminded herself that they were to be colleagues, nothing more, and there was no reason for her to get out there and personal about the man.

Yet, minutes later, when Vicki tapped on her door, popped her head in and said, 'Dr McNeal's here,' Jo sprang to her feet as if a fire-cracker had gone off in her consulting room.

'He apologises for being a bit early,' Vicki said. 'And guess what?' The receptionist's voice rose to an excited squeak.

Jo blinked. 'What?'

'He's got his baby with him!'

A baby. *A baby!* Brady McNeal had a baby, when all the time she'd thought of his son in terms of kindergarten age, a little boy of three or four. But a *baby*.

'Come on.' Vicki was beckoning enthusiastically. 'He's adorable.'

Almost dazedly, Jo followed Vicki along the corridor to Reception, only to find Marika and Monica and even several of the female patients from the waiting room gathered in a fluttering little huddle to admire baby McNeal, who was gazing up, wide-eyed, from his carry-capsule.

Oh, lord. Jo swallowed. They'd all gone mad. She felt like clapping her hands like the nuns from her school days to restore some order to the surgery.

But she didn't. Instead, she found a tiny gap in the circle and looked down at the baby boy.

And fell instantly in love.

Oh, my... Jo clenched a hand over her heart, marvelling at the completeness of him, the utter perfection of tiny fingers, cute little ears and button nose. A rush of very mixed emotions engulfed her and words she wasn't even aware of saying tumbled out. 'Aren't you beautiful?'

'Ooh…' Collective female sighs went round the circle. 'He's smiling.'

'He likes you, Jo.' Vicki squeezed her arm, her expression all soft and mushy. 'Just look at him, the pet…'

Jo looked. And looked again. And then got a grip on herself. She tugged Monica aside. 'Where's Dr McNeal now?'

'Tying up the paperwork with Angelo,' Monica said absently, her gaze winging back to the baby as if drawn by an invisible thread. She sighed reminiscently. 'We haven't had a baby in the practice since Jane and Riley left with their little Kiara Rose.'

All that had been before her time. Jo looked distractedly around. The baby was lovely but this was supposed to be a medical practice, not a crèche. Someone had to break up the party.

'Right, let's get back to work, everyone.' Surprisingly, it was Vicki, taking over and sounding quite professional about it. 'Dr Rutherford, I have you all set up in the staffroom. So let's get this little guy back to his dad, shall we?' So saying, she gathered up the capsule by its handles and wafted ahead of Jo along the corridor.

Feeling pulled every which way, Jo turned, following a pace behind. She felt in shock. Almost. And nothing was going to plan. Nothing. Who could she get to look after a baby full time? A *baby*.

She didn't have much time to think about it. From his consulting room at the other end of the corridor, Angelo emerged with Brady. Their heads were turned towards each other and they were obviously deep in conversation.

And they hadn't seen her. Thanking all the saints in heaven, Jo darted ahead of Vicki into the staffroom, holding the door open for her to angle the capsule through. And berating herself for her loony behaviour. She should have waited beside the door and greeted Brady politely and professionally. Instead, she went to the window and looked out—at nothing.

'Come on, now, pumpkin.' Expertly, Vicki lifted the baby from his capsule. 'Let's go meet your daddy, shall we? Just buzz me if you need anything, Jo.'

'Thanks…I will,' Jo croaked.

It was only a few seconds then until Angelo and Brady

McNeal stopped at the open doorway. Seconds when Jo felt every nerve-end stretched tightly.

'Jo will look after you now,' she heard Angelo say, and then Brady had taken a step inside and Jo turned to face him, her arms linked defensively across her midriff. She blinked and something shifted inside her as she took in the tender picture of Brady and his infant son.

He held him close, tucked into the crook of his arm, one large, masculine hand cradling his son's tiny feet. And they looked so right together. Already a family. Jo felt a wash of emotion she couldn't explain.

'Jo.' Brady's mouth made a brief twist of acknowledgement.

'Hello, Brady.' She gave a stilted laugh. 'This is all a bit odd, isn't it? I mean, the way we met and neither of us knowing we were about to become work colleagues.'

'Maybe it *was* kismet, then?'

Fate? Maybe it was and maybe it wasn't. She gave him a taut smile.

Brady's gaze sharpened. 'Angelo put me right about everything. So, no surprises and no harm done. And it *is* good to see you again. I'm sure we'll work well together, aren't you?'

Jo nodded. 'Of course.' It would have been entirely unprofessional to have said otherwise. 'Shall we get settled, then? I believe you're going to need some child care.'

'Ah…yes.' Brady shifted his weight slightly as he turned and placed his son back in his capsule. 'What are my chances, do you think?'

'Not sure, really,' Jo said. They pulled out chairs and made themselves comfortable at one end of the long table. 'For some reason, I expected an older child.'

Brady frowned and she guessed he was puzzled by her assumption. 'I don't recall I gave that impression at the interview.'

'No...well...' Jo lifted a shoulder dismissively. 'It's immaterial now. Let's get a few details, shall we? How old is the baby?'

'AJ is six months.'

'AJ?' Jo's eyes widened in query.

'Andrew James,' Brady enlightened. 'I named him after my father and grandfather. But we shortened it to save confusion. I wouldn't have brought him with me today, except for a few unforeseen circumstances. Normally my mother would have been able to take care of him, but unfortunately she had other commitments today.'

Jo absorbed the information with a nod. 'Do you need to give Andrew a bottle or anything?'

'No...' Brady's look softened. 'He's not due for a while.'

Jo looked thoughtful. He *seemed* at ease in his role of sole parent, but surely there would have been times, like now, for instance, when he must feel the strain of it. Something propelled her to say, 'It must have been a bit hair-raising, embarking on the long flight from Canada with such a young child.'

His eyes glinted and a quick frown marked his forehead. 'Your point being?'

Jo was taken aback. He was almost bristling with defensiveness. Obviously he thought she was questioning his capability as a parent. Well, if he chose to take things the wrong way, that was his problem. She hadn't wanted to be put in this position of trying to organise his child care.

She pinned his gaze, her own firing green sparks. 'I'm not making any particular *point*. The only concern I have is for Andrew's care to go smoothly. Can I take it you're the one making the decisions?'

He huffed a bitter laugh. 'If you're worried his mother will turn up and cause a ruckus with the arrangements, don't. Tanya is out of the picture. I have legal custody of my son.'

Jo was shocked at the sudden locked-down expression on his face, and her own anger vanished like leaves in the wind. The man was obviously toting a massive load of emotional baggage.

In a split second she wondered why on earth she felt the insane desire to help him carry it.

But before she could form any words, Brady dropped back in his chair with a muted 'Oh, hell.' Stabbing a hand through his hair, he met her eyes with a crooked and repentant smile. 'I didn't mean to snap at you, Jo. Can we start again?'

She hesitated a moment, her even white teeth rolling over the corner of her bottom lip, unable to believe the sudden crazy need she felt to make things right for him and his son. 'Fine with me.'

His 'Thank you' was heartfelt, and as Jo looked at him across the desk, their eyes met and held and she felt the instant shock of it shimmer right up her spine.

Sweet God. Brady blinked and blinked again. It was like being struck by lightning. Silver-green lightning, lancing through him and anchoring him to the chair. With a little grimace he dragged his eyes away and gave himself a mental kick in the backside. This was no time to be indulging in fantasies. For now his priorities had to be elsewhere, with his baby...

'So,' Jo was asking, 'are you expecting any separation trauma when you have to leave your son?'

He slammed back to reality. 'For my part, certainly. I'll

miss him like crazy. But AJ should be fine. He's been in and out of child care practically since day one. If all else fails and I can't get a carer, my mother will come down in a temporary capacity until I get things sorted. My work won't suffer,' he added tersely.

Did it appear as though she'd thought otherwise? He'd wrong-footed her again but she ploughed on. 'I don't imagine you'd have taken the job without considering all the implications. And there may be someone suitable…'

He lifted a hand, his fingers scraping roughly over his chin. 'Sorry if I appear abrasive about this. I don't mean to be.'

With a twitch of her shoulder, Jo shrugged off his apology. 'Let's just concentrate on getting a successful outcome for Andrew, shall we?'

He leaned forward earnestly. 'I really want to make this work. The practice seems just what I've been looking for in terms of location and workload, and the town itself is a real gem.'

Jo got right on her hobby-horse. 'I love it here,' she confessed. 'Have you had a good look around?'

'Mmm.' More relaxed now, Brady settled back in his chair. 'The day I came for the interview. I was amazed to find that old-world department store in the main street.'

'Geraldo's. Incredible, isn't it? Been there since the early nineteen hundreds apparently.'

'And I was intrigued by their motto above the front door…' Brady's eyes narrowed as he tried to remember it.

'"We sell everything from wagon wheels to watermelons",' Jo supplied with a soft laugh. 'But I doubt if they sell watermelons these days. There's an excellent co-op fruit mart here now.'

'And a library and art gallery as well.' Brady added to the list. 'The hospital isn't half bad either.'

Jo smiled wryly at that. 'It has its ups and downs, staff-wise. If you've any expertise in any particular discipline, they'll rope you in.'

'I've done some anaesthetics,' Brady said modestly.

'You didn't want to specialise?'

'Not really. I much prefer my patients awake and talking. What about you? What do they rope you in for?'

'I've some experience in paeds.'

He nodded. 'So, would you be prepared to take AJ onto your list?'

She should have seen that coming. Jo gave a half-smile. 'Seeing you're a colleague... I take it he's up to date with his shots and so on?'

'Yes, Doctor.'

Jo made a face at him. 'Dads are notorious for forgetting those small details,' she said lightly.

'But, then, I think we've established I'm no ordinary dad, am I?'

No. She guessed Brady McNeal wasn't. He appeared to have taken on the Herculean task of being both mother and father to his baby boy. But she didn't want to go there. There had to be some deep emotional issues swirling around in his past. Very deep. She guessed time would tell whether he would ever be prepared to share them.

'The lady I have in mind for Andrew is Thea Williams.' Jo dragged the interview back on track. 'She normally does fostering or emergency care for kids who for some reason can't be with their parents. But I know she was the carer for my predecessor's baby when she wanted to return to work part time. And according to the staff here, Dr Rossiter was very pleased with her.'

Brady's eyes lit with interest. 'Your Thea Williams sounds ideal. But I would prefer to keep AJ in his own surroundings, if possible. Would she come to my home each day?'

'That shouldn't be a problem. From Thea's point of view, it would be more practical anyway.'

'And save *me* a mad dash in the mornings, I dare say,' he said with a rueful grin. 'So, I guess the sixty-four-thousand dollar question is would Mrs Williams be prepared to work overtime when I'm on call? I understand from Angelo we do weekend cover at the after-hours clinic on a rotational basis.'

Jo nodded. 'It's a fairly recent adjunct to the district, partly funded by the local council. There are several MOs who come in from surrounding areas as well. So, we're really committed only every four weeks or so.'

'Sounds pretty reasonable.'

'As for whether Thea will agree to work occasional longer hours, I'll ring her now and put that to her,' Jo said. 'If she's happy about the arrangements in general, you'd probably be best to go round to her place so she can meet you and the baby.'

'I'll pay over the going rate,' Brady put forward hopefully, as if that might secure Thea's services.

'Well, let's just see first, shall we? You mightn't take to one another at all,' Jo reminded him.

He smiled then, a little half-smile that seemed to flicker on one side of his lips before settling into place. 'I trust you, Dr Rutherford, to steer me right.' And with that he got to his feet. 'I'll hang about in Reception while you make your call. OK if I leave AJ here with you?'

Jo nodded and rose from her chair as well and they both stood looking down at Andrew James McNeal. A long exquisite sigh passed from the baby's rosebud mouth as he slept, causing Jo to murmur involuntarily, 'He's a beautiful child, isn't he?'

'I think so…' Brady leaned over and with protective male tenderness gently stroked his son's cheek with the tip of his middle finger.

'Oh, I forgot to ask.' Jo's hand went to the silver chain at her throat. 'Have you found somewhere to live?'

'I have.' His voice was deep and almost detached. 'It's a cottage, already furnished—just what I was looking for.'

CHAPTER THREE

MONDAY morning.

Brady came quietly into the staffroom to begin his first day as a family practitioner at Mt Pryde Medical Centre. His 'Good morning' was met with an answering chorus from the other staff members.

He helped himself to a coffee from the filter machine. Then, mug in hand, he stood with his back against the wall and almost bemusedly watched his colleagues as they eased themselves into their working day.

Tom, who had obviously missed breakfast, was making himself toast and Marmite at the benchtop. Angelo was looking through his mail and grumbling to anyone who would listen that it was about time specialists got off their collective tails and came to rural hospitals to conduct clinics.

While Jo... And there Brady stopped, his gaze skimming her slender figure, lingering on the pristine little top that showed off her tan from her recent holiday and then dropping to run the length of her legs in their soft cotton trousers. Then back to her silver-blonde head, bent over a journal of some kind while she almost absently took a mouthful of coffee from the mug in her left hand.

Brady's heart thumped against his ribs. He should really ask her round for a meal. She'd done so much to help him settle in. And matching him up with Thea was proving a godsend. He could come to the surgery each day knowing his son was in the best of hands.

Guilt and need in equal measure gnawed at him. He could ask Jo round tonight—knock together a pasta of some description. Then he stopped his train of thought abruptly. He couldn't involve her in his life outside the practice. He'd chosen to walk this path alone. And that's the way it had to stay.

Vicki breezed in. 'Hi, everyone.'

'Hi, Vic,' was the chorused reply.

Vicki made her way across to the bench and with no attempt at subtlety elbowed Tom out of way. 'I hope you're intending to clean up after yourself, young Dr Yardley?'

Tom stuffed a corner of toast into his mouth. 'I thought you might, Vic…'

'In your dreams, sunshine. I've my own work to do. Brady.' She dimpled a smile back over her shoulder. 'Ready for your first day?'

'Just about.' Brady took another mouthful of his coffee. 'Can anyone tell me why people assume that doctors in general survive on casseroles?'

'Come again?' Angelo's dark head came up and he blinked.

Brady gave a twitch of his shoulders. 'I've already had three given to me, one from my elderly neighbour and *two* from a nice lady who called yesterday and said she was from the church.'

'No one gave me casseroles when I moved into my place,' Tom grumbled.

'You only eat pizzas,' Vicki scolded. 'You'd have chucked them out.'

'Would not. I'd have given them to the poor of the parish.'

'Oh, for Pete's sake, children!' Angelo shook his head and got to his feet. He scooped up the rest of his mail. 'Folk here are friendly, Brady. News of your arrival will have travelled fast. And the fact you have a baby, well...'

Brady's mouth turned up in a wry grin. 'You mean I can expect gifts of nappies and formula as well?'

That remark brought laughter. Then a general exodus began.

Jo had been conscious of Brady from the second he'd walked into the staffroom. She just hoped things worked out for him in Mt Pryde and he'd want to stay.

She didn't ask herself why she wanted that. Didn't dare. Instead, she realised she'd have to keep reminding herself she had to work with him, had to treat him as a colleague and not allow her senses to zoom to full alert every time he came within her orbit.

She hung back purposely, waiting for everyone to clear the room. But Brady was still there, washing his mug at the sink. She glanced at her watch. She had to get on. Slipping off the high stool where she'd been perched, she asked, 'How was Andrew this morning?'

Brady upended his mug on the drainer and began to dry his hands on a paper towel. 'Good. Thea has great plans for them today.'

'You could slip home at lunchtime and make sure he's all right.'

Brady's mouth twitched briefly. 'I'm tempted—but, no, I don't want to start being distracted from my job. That's not fair to the rest of the team.'

'Just till you and AJ settle in.'

He shook his head. 'It's kind of you to suggest it, Jo, but let me do this my way—OK?'

Jo's mouth flattened in an apologetic smile. 'It was just a thought.'

'I know.' His own smile was teasing and very direct. 'It's probably your mothering instincts at play.'

Jo felt her face warm. Now, there was a thought. 'Uh, has Ralph handed over to you yet?'

'Mmm. I spent the entire day here with him yesterday.'

Sunday? Jo frowned. 'That was a bit above the call of duty, wasn't it?'

He shrugged. 'I didn't mind. Especially in the circumstances.'

So Ralph had obviously told him about his grandson. 'It's a real blow for the family.'

'I'd be completely gutted if anything like that happened to AJ,' Brady replied soberly. Then in a beat his mood lightened and he moved to the door and held it open for her. 'Come on, Dr Rutherford, or Vicki will be after our hides.'

Jo made a face. 'Mondays are always nuts, aren't they?'

'Yep. But I'm really looking forward to meeting my patients and getting stuck in.'

'Just yell if you need to consult about anything,' Jo offered.

'Thanks, Jo—for *everything*.' For what seemed like aeons they held each other's gaze and Brady felt his throat constrict. Her eyes were like emerald-green pools, inviting him to dive in.

Oh, damn. If only he dared.

He cleared his throat. 'Uh, probably see you at lunch-time, then.'

She nodded and they turned, each heading in opposite directions to their consulting rooms.

With a feeling of optimism Brady picked up the card for his first patient from Vicki, then stuck his head into the waiting room and called, 'Samara? Come through, please.'

A young woman in jeans and skinny-rib top rose to her feet. 'You're new, aren't you?' she said, click-clacking along in her sandals behind him and then taking the chair beside his desk.

'Brady McNeal. I'm taking over Dr Mitchell's patients.'

Samara, who was nineteen, pressed her hands together prayer-like, locking them between her jeans-clad knees. 'I've had some tests done. Dr Mitchell said he'd have the results if I came back today.'

'That's right.' Brady had gone carefully over the young woman's notes with Ralph.

Originally, she'd presented with chronic fatigue and lethargy, and after several attempts to get at the cause of her problems with no worthwhile results, Ralph had sent her for a small bowel gastroscopy—a biopsy of the small intestine. The results were back and, bingo!

Brady brought up her file on the computer. 'The results of your biopsy are pretty conclusive, Samara,' he told his patient gently. 'It appears you have what is known as coeliac disease.' He spelled it out for her and said, 'It's pronounced, *seal-e-ack*.'

Samara shook her head. 'I don't understand. What does it mean exactly?'

'In simple terms,' Brady said, 'it means you have an intolerance to gluten.'

'That's wheat and stuff, isn't it?'

Brady nodded. 'Especially wheat, but we can't dismiss other grains like rye, barley and possibly oats.'

Samara chewed her bottom lip, digesting the information. 'So what will I eat, then? I mean, there are additives in everything these days. Will I have to start reading every label on every bit of food I buy? That'll be a real pain. I live away from home,' she expanded, 'so it's not like I can get my mum to prepare my food.'

'It will be a bit of a minefield,' Brady agreed. 'But don't lose heart before you start. Just think that if it's going to make the difference between you feeling well or not well, it'll be worth doing, won't it?'

'I guess…'

He smiled reassuringly and pulled a couple of pamphlets from his drawer. 'You won't have to do it all on your own. There's quite an active support group in the town. But read these for a start and I'll give you a letter of referral to the dietitian at the hospital. Make an appointment as soon as you can. She'll have a fund of information you'll be able to tap into.'

Samara took the pamphlets and looked down at them. 'Looks like I'll have to be really picky about what I eat,' she said glumly.

'If it's to be of benefit to you, the diet has to be strict,' Brady pointed out practically. 'But don't imagine you'll have to go on army rations. There will be a vast range of foods you'll be able to eat. And enjoy. You'll just have a different eating pattern from most of us, that's all.'

Samara swept a hand through her white-blonde fringe,

leaving it in little tufts. 'So when I get going with this new diet, I should start to feel better, shouldn't I?'

'You should.' Brady was cautious. 'But it may be slow and gradual. You'll begin to notice your energy picking up. That'll be a good sign. Give your new diet a month or so and then come back and we'll test your iron levels. That will be an indicator that you're on the right track.'

Samara's pretty mouth flattened in resignation. 'Bang go my ham and pineapple pizzas, then. The bases are all made from wheat flour for sure. And toast! I love my toast!'

'Hang on.' Brady raised a hand in a halting motion. 'Maybe not…' He picked up his phone and depressed the number he'd memorised. 'Ah, Jo, sorry to bother you.' He explained why he was calling and listened for a moment. 'Thanks for that,' he said, before clipping the receiver back on its cradle. 'Samara, you're in luck.' His head came up and he smiled. 'Apparently the baker in the arcade makes a gluten-free bread for special customers, but you'll need to order it in advance.'

A tiny dimple flickered in Samara's cheek. 'So I can have my toast?'

'Probably.' Brady handed the referral letter to his patient and got to his feet to see her out. 'But to be on the safe side, perhaps run it past the dietitian when you see her, OK?'

Brady ploughed on through his patient list, pleased he'd got through by one o'clock when the surgery officially closed for lunch.

He was feeling reasonably upbeat about his morning. He'd managed pretty well, he decided, and had coped without bugging his colleagues too much. Except for his query to Jo, he'd only had to double-check the name of a drug with Angelo before he'd prescribed it. In Canada the drug in question had been dispensed under another brand name entirely. Much better to make sure.

Tom and Jo were already in the staffroom when Brady made his way in. 'Still in one piece, mate?' Tom quipped, his nose buried in the sports section of the local paper.

'And intending to stay that way,' Brady quipped back. 'Thanks for your help earlier, by the way.' He turned towards Jo, who was trying to find the beginning of a new roll of clingfilm.

'That's OK. Oh!' With a yelp of frustration she thrust the lot at Brady. 'See if you can get it started. It hates me!'

He chuckled and took the offending box of cling film. 'About lunch,' he said, painstakingly setting about unravelling the mangled film. 'Do we bring our own or what?'

'We do a communal thing,' Jo said. 'Vicki collects money from us each week and then shops for fresh bread and various sandwich fillings. Just help yourself to anything in the fridge.'

Intent on his task, Brady continued, 'So I pay Vicki, then?'

Tom sniggered. 'She'll hunt you down, mate. Never fear. Jo, are you doing me a sandwich?'

'I wouldn't think so.'

Tom got up and peered over her shoulder at the cutting board. 'So, who're the extra slices for, then?'

'Brady—because he's new.'

'I'm still new,' Tom protested.

'Rats,' Jo said mildly. 'You've been here for over a year.' Still smiling, she swung a look back over her shoulder. 'Brady, turkey, avocado and cos lettuce OK?'

'Sounds very healthy.' Brady had the clingfilm running smoothly and placed it back on the worktop.

'The tomatoes in the basket are from Monica's garden.' Jo said conversationally. 'Her husband, Terry, grows acid-free beauties. She supplies us with heaps.' With quick, neat movements Jo made his sandwich, slipped it onto a plate and handed it across to him. 'Enjoy.'

'Thanks.' He eyed her levelly. 'I'll make yours tomorrow.'

Jo managed to hold his gaze more or less steadily. 'Don't make rash promises,' she warned lightly. 'There's bound to be an emergency or three around the corner.'

Jo's last patient for the day was Leisa Cooper. She worked at the local library and was pregnant with her first child.

'How are you feeling?' Jo asked, when Leisa sank gratefully into the chair.

'Awful,' Leisa confessed. 'I feel so darned tired already and I have weeks to go. And I'm thirsty all the time and having to pee twice as much.'

Jo's medical instincts sharpened. 'How long has this been going on?'

'Not long. It just feels long.' She made a small face. 'Couple of weeks, I suppose. Is that significant?'

'Could be.' Jo wound the blood-pressure cuff around her patient's arm and took a reading. And made a swift decision. 'I'm going to send you along for a glucose tolerance test, Leisa. I'd like you go first thing tomorrow, if possible.'

Leisa's head came up, her eyes wide in alarm. 'Is something wrong with me?'

'Nothing drastically,' Jo reassured her patient gently. 'But you may be developing something called gestational diabetes. And before you get too worried, the condition is quite common in pregnancy.'

'Is it something I've done wrong?'

'Nothing like that. While you're pregnant, the placenta is busily secreting hormones but in some women the uptake of hormones increases the body's resistance to insulin. When this happens, you need more insulin to help the body's cells and muscles take up glucose from the bloodstream.'

Leisa touched a hand to her tummy. 'So, what happens?'

'Simply, the glucose stays around in the bloodstream. That's why we need the test done, to see what's going on with you.' Jo took up her pen to write out the request for the path lab. 'It would be helpful if you could have the morning off to have this GTT done, Leisa.'

'I could probably arrange that.' Leisa looked thoughtful for a moment. 'So, how involved is this glucose tolerance test, then?'

'Not terribly,' Jo said. 'It just takes a while. First off, you'll be asked to drink a quantity of Lucosade.'

'My poor bladder,' Leisa groaned. 'I won't have to drink gallons of the stuff, will I?'

Jo chuckled. 'No. From memory, the amount is around three hundred mils. After that, your blood will be tested at one hourly intervals, three in all. If your blood glucose levels indicate you're not within the normal range, we'll begin treatment.'

'Oh, lord…' Leisa sighed. 'Is the rest of my pregnancy going to be awful?'

Jo shook her head. 'Don't think like that, Leisa. I'd hope diet and exercise will get things right for you. If the diagnosis in confirmed, we'll begin liaising with Vanessa Rowntree, the dietitian at the hospital. She'll do an intensive medical history with you and then get you started on an appropriate health regime.'

Leisa's mouth turned down. 'I must admit I don't get a lot of exercise, sitting on my backside in the library.'

'Well, some walks might be in order, then,' Jo said brightly. 'Hop out of bed earlier in the morning and get Troy to go with you. I promise, you'll both feel a lot healthier for it.'

'I saw Dr Yardley for my check-up while you were away,' Leisa said. 'Shouldn't he have noticed if something was wrong?'

'Not necessarily.' Jo was quick to defend Tom's medical credentials. 'Gestational diabetes usually manifests itself somewhere between twenty-six and twenty-eight weeks. And you're just on the twenty-eight week mark, which coincidentally is exactly the right time for this GTT to be done.'

Leisa gave a wry laugh. 'I thought I'd whiz through pregnancy. With hindsight, perhaps we should have started our family earlier...'

'Starting off in our twenties does seem to be the current consensus for women,' Jo agreed, and thought her own age was creeping up as well. But if you didn't have a special man to have a baby with, there wasn't much point in agonising about your declining fertility. 'If it turns out you do have gestational diabetes, we'll monitor you carefully.'

'Thanks, Jo.' Leisa looked more cheerful. 'I feel better knowing you've got a handle on things.'

'I'm your doctor.' Jo smiled. 'That's my job. Just as it's your job to deliver a healthy babe. Now, let's do the fun part, shall we? Pop up on the couch and we'll see if junior is progressing nicely.'

CHAPTER FOUR

WITH a muted sigh Jo lifted the phone to make the last call on her list. It had been one of their busiest weeks. Punching in the numbers, she wondered briefly how Brady had coped. She'd caught up with him only fleetingly.

The week had had some positives, though, Jo reflected. That morning she'd been able to reassure Nora Burows that her lesion was benign.

Glancing at her watch, she realised she'd just about make it in time for their Friday staff meeting—that's if her party on the other end of the line answered some time before next Christmas...

'Right, people, if no one has any further business, that's it.' Angelo pocketed his pen and shot an enquiring glance at his partners. 'Brady, your patient load OK?'

'No complaints.' Brady rolled his shoulders and stretched.

'Don't forget it's Ralph's farewell party at my place tomorrow evening,' Angelo reminded them as he got to his feet. 'Sixish OK with everyone?'

A murmur of agreement.

'Do you need a hand with anything?' Jo asked.

Angelo's white teeth glinted in a smile. 'Thanks, Jo, but

Pen has a rare weekend off so we're up and running. Oh, Brady, you won't know where to find our place. It's out of town a bit.' He felt in his pocket to retrieve his pen.

Jo flapped a hand. 'I'll do the necessary, Angelo. You take off.'

'Thanks.' He shot her a grateful smile. 'I want to catch the butcher before he closes. Have to collect our steaks for tomorrow. 'Night, all.'

''Night,' they echoed.

'That's me as well, guys.' Tom shot back his chair. 'There's a big beautiful weekend out there and I'm off to grab me a hunk of it. See you both at the barbecue.' He sketched a wave as he shot out the door.

Jo and Brady exchanged pained looks. 'I can't re-member being that young,' Brady said ruefully, gathering up his notes. 'Or so enthusiastic about a weekend, for that matter.'

Jo suppressed a giggle. 'Knees creaking a bit, are they?'

He mock-swiped her with a manila folder. 'Wait till you have a baby giving you the runaround at night, Doctor.'

'Oh, poor you. Is it that bad?'

'I'll survive.' A gleam of wry humour lurked in his eyes. 'Takes me back to the sleep deprivation of the intern years.'

They left the surgery together. 'Oh, Angelo's place…' Jo had remembered suddenly. 'Do you have a pen handy? I'll draw you a map, shall I?'

Brady stopped by his car, flicking the remote to open the locks and stowing his medical case in the boot. 'Better still, why don't I pick you up tomorrow evening and you can show me the way personally?'

Jo felt a thread of uncertainty. And hesitated. 'Best if I take my own car, I think,' she responded, forcing a smile.

'We'd be saving petrol,' Brady countered practically.

And setting everyone speculating.

In an awkward little movement Jo swung her medical case in front of her, locking one hand on top of the other. 'Perhaps some other time, Brady.'

'You're right, of course.' A muscle flickered in his jaw. Idiot. She probably had a boyfriend. Hell, with her looks, she probably had several. He swallowed the lump of disappointment in his throat. 'I apologise for making assumptions. If you'd just give me general directions to Angelo's…?'

Now he'd taken offence. A tiny frown pleated her forehead. She guessed he was lonely to some extent. Well, of course, he would be. And housebound with the baby, doubly so.

Jo ached inside for him. 'Look, there's no reason why we can't wind down a bit after our working week. Why don't you go home, collect AJ and come to me for a meal?'

'Easier if you came to me.' Brady felt relief whip through him. Perhaps she didn't have a boyfriend after all. 'Makes sense.' He shot her a coaxing half-smile. 'That way, I can leave the baby undisturbed.'

Well, of course it made sense. But go to his place? Be alone with him? The only word that sprang into her head was intimacy. Were either of them ready for that?

On the other hand, how could she refuse when he looked so darned needy? And more sexy than he had any right to be. Well, she could handle that. Just. She tipped him a dry look in capitulation. 'I'll shoot home first to shower and change, and grab a take-away of some kind on my way to you.'

'No, don't do that. I'll cook.'

She flipped him a cheeky grin. 'You can, I take it?'

'Sure.' He lifted a shoulder in a shrug. 'I do a mean pasta.'

* * *

A ripple of lightness mixed with a new kind of awareness shimmied through Jo as she dressed in white cargo pants and a black and white T-shirt that skimmed her curves and ended snugly at her waist. Her complexion, still glowing with the soft tan from her holiday, needed no more than a dash of moisturiser. And she couldn't be bothered with lipstick, preferring the natural look whenever she could get away with it.

After all, it was just a casual meal with a colleague, she reminded herself a few minutes later as she secured her hair in a butterfly clip, snatched up her keys and made her way out to the carport.

The drive to Brady's house took barely minutes. Dove Street was in a nice part of the town, Jo thought, with lots of trees and well-kept footpaths. She was glad he'd found such a pretty cottage, too.

She parked neatly in the driveway, slid out and pocketed her keys. Taking a deep breath, she walked across the strip of lawn and mounted the shallow steps that led onto the front verandah.

Ringing the doorbell, she turned and crossed to the railings, admiring the tumbling array of small perennials that bordered the path and the big old mango tree that was crying out for a swing to be placed on one of its sturdy lower branches. Well, perhaps in time AJ would get to play on it. One day. If Brady was still in the vicinity...

She spun round, her heart leaping when the door opened. Brady's name died on her lips for it was Thea who'd opened the door. 'Thea,' she said faintly.

'Jo.' The older woman's plump face was wreathed in a welcoming smile. 'Brady said it would be you. Come on through. We're in the kitchen—or I am, at least. Brady's just finishing Andrew's bath.'

It sound so utterly domestic, Jo thought, feeling slightly foolish at her wild assumption that Brady had been planning an intimate kind of evening for just the two of them.

She gave a tiny rueful laugh. It seemed she'd misread all those silent little messages his eyes had been sending out almost since they'd met. At least she knew where she stood with him now.

She shoved her heart back into its rightful place.

'Are you working late this evening?' Jo took a cursory look around. Thea had obviously just completed a baking session and was putting bowls and beaters away in their respective homes.

'Not me.' Thea laughed, whipping off her apron and hanging it behind the door. 'Brady would never hear of it. The thing is, it's my choir night and it's closer to the church hall from here. Saves me going all the way home and then having to come back. And don't imagine Brady has asked me to cook, Jo.' Thea homed in on Jo's misgivings accurately. 'When the little one is asleep, I have lots of spare time. And I may as well be useful.'

Jo threw the older woman an apologetic smile. 'I wasn't meaning to question your role here, Thea. That's strictly between you and Brady.'

'Rest assured, I love it here. Ah…' Thea turned her head and smiled. 'That sounds like the men now.'

And then the McNeal males were upon them, Andrew riding high in the crook of his father's arm.

'Jo.' Brady sent her a measured smile. 'You made it, then?'

Jo nodded, feeling her heart flip over. They looked so right together, father and son, a little family unit. She watched, her expression soft, as Brady almost absently rubbed his cheek against the baby's downy head. And then without even realising what she was doing, Jo put out her hands towards the little blue-clad bundle. 'May I hold him?'

Brady's expression was unreadable as he handed the child over. Then he spun away, bracing his hands on the back of a kitchen chair. 'Thea, what time do you need to be out of here?'

'Half an hour or so. I could give Andrew his bottle, if you like, and you and Jo can get on with your dinner preparations.'

'Sounds good. OK with you, Jo?' He straightened, his hands going to his lean hips as he looked quizzically down at her.

Jo's hold tightened on the baby in her arms. She didn't want to give him up, she realised, catching the little starfish hand he waved in playful contentment. And how crazy was that? 'Yes, fine,' she murmured, placing the softest kiss on the infant's head, before handing him over to Thea.

'I'll help but I'm not doing the onions,' Jo declared, as Brady assembled the ingredients for their pasta dish.

'Did anyone ask you to, Doctor?' Brady's look was droll. 'Just relax and watch me.'

She gave a throaty chuckle. 'Show-off.'

'Just practical,' Brady countered, moving her gently to one side while he set up the cutting board. 'Get yourself a glass of wine and relax. There's a nice white open in the fridge.'

'I assume you're having one?' Jo had located the wine and found the glasses.

'Yes, please.' He skinned the onions and began chopping them, very fast.

Jo blinked. 'That's very impressive. I kept expecting to

see the tops of a couple of fingers mingling with the finished product.'

'Now, there's a thought. We could save on the tomato sauce.' He grinned, touching her glass with his.

'You seem to be settling in nicely.' Jo had taken a liberal mouthful of her wine and made herself comfortable on one of the high-backed kitchen stools.

Brady moved to the sink and washed his hands quickly. 'I guess I've taken the right fork in the road this time,' he said candidly. 'Ever been faced with those kinds of decisions?'

'What—forks in the road?' Jo considered his question for a moment. 'Probably everyone has at some time. But speaking for myself, nothing so serious I couldn't have turned back if I'd wanted to.'

'That's good to hear…' Brady leaned across the counter and knuckled her cheek playfully, his eyes so close to hers she could see the little flecks of black in the brown.

'Nice wine.' Jo dropped her gaze quickly, a shiver of awareness shafting through her with the touch of his skin on hers.

Oh, boy. Brady turned abruptly, opening the pantry and peering blankly inside. Every time he looked at her he ached to touch her intimately, to stroke the smoothness of her skin, to kiss the tiny hollow at the base of her throat, breathe in the sweet scent of her hair.

But he didn't want to be noticing these things, did he?

Good grief! After the kick in the guts Tanya had landed on him, you'd think he'd have had more sense than to be so eager to trust a woman again. Any woman…

'Doctor! Dr McNeal?' There was a sharp rapping on Brady's back door and a woman's agitated voice asking, 'Please—are you there?'

Brady swung to Jo, his expression immediately alert. 'That's my neighbour, Ellen Farmer.'

'Sounds like trouble.' Jo climbed off the high stool and hurried after him.

Brady flung open the door, catching the elderly woman as she almost fell inside. 'Ellen—what is it? It's OK. Just tell me what's happened,' he said gently, when Ellen began trembling uncontrollably.

'It's Lester…'

'Yes, your husband…' Brady nodded. 'Is he hurt?'

'He's cut his hand on the band-saw. There's a big piece of flesh hanging off.' Ellen went deathly pale. 'He's bleeding.'

'Right.' Brady pushed her into a chair. 'Is he in his workshop in the back garden?'

Ellen nodded. 'I ran to get you…'

'That's good, Ellen. You did the right thing. We'll look after him now. I'll get my bag.' Brady turned urgently to Jo. 'I'll just ask Thea to hang on a bit.'

Jo nodded. 'I've a small cylinder of oxygen in my medical kit. I'll collect it from the car and go next door. Meet you there.'

'Great. Thanks. Be as quick as you can,' he said in an undertone. 'Lester's an old chap. God knows what we'll find.'

When Brady returned to the kitchen, Ellen was back on her feet. 'I'm coming with you, Doctor,' she said determinedly.

Brady didn't argue.

They found Lester on the floor of the shed, his back braced against the wall, his hand wrapped tightly in one of the dust rags he used on his machines. He was very pale and obviously in shock. 'Must be gettin' old,' he said weakly as Brady hunkered down beside him. 'Piece of wood was too heavy—pulled me hand into the saw. Should have seen it coming.'

'Take it easy, Lester,' Brady said gently. 'Accidents happen.' He put his case down and snapped open the locks. 'This is Dr Rutherford from the practice,' he introduced Jo. 'She's going to pop an oxygen mask on you. It will help you over the shock you're feeling. Just breathe away now. That's the way.'

'Better now. Thanks, Doc.' Lester closed his eyes.

'Will he be all right?' Ellen hovered tearfully. 'Can I help at all?'

'Yes, you can, Ellen.' Jo drew her aside. 'We need to know if Lester is on any medication.'

'Well, we both are. I mean, as you age, you— Sorry.' She took a calming breath. 'He's on warfarin.'

Jo sent an urgent look to Brady and he nodded almost imperceptibly. The drug was an anti-clotting agent. They had double trouble.

Gently, Brady unwound the rag and took a careful look at the elderly man's wound. His mouth drew in. Lester had almost sliced his thumb off. He was going to need surgery. At least it was a clean cut, but there was certainly nerve and tissue damage. And once the pressure had been eased, the hand had begun bleeding profusely.

Ellen hovered, watching Brady apply a compression bandage to Lester's wound. 'He looks so frail,' she said, knotting her hands across her chest in agitation.

'He'll be all right, Ellen,' Brady said kindly, and mentally crossed his fingers. 'But he'll have to go to hospital. In the meantime, we need to elevate his injured hand. Would you have a large piece of material we could use as a sling—an old sheet, perhaps? Curtaining—anything.'

'I've some cot sheets from the grandchildren.' Ellen took off, seeming pleased to be doing something to help her husband. At the door of the shed she paused and looked back. 'Should I call the ambulance?'

Brady looked a question at Jo. 'What are our chances this time on a Friday?'

'Probably not great. For some reason everything starts to go pear-shaped before the weekend.'

'We won't hang about, then. Ellen, I'll take you and Lester across to the casualty department. The sooner a surgeon can look at that hand, the better.'

'We should get some fluids into him, Brady.' With Ellen temporarily absent, Jo felt free to tell it as it was. And she was concerned about the tell-tale moistness of the elderly man's skin. 'Do you have saline with you?'

'Yup. Hook him up, will you? Meanwhile I'll give him a jab of morphine. He's got to be in some pain.'

Jo worked quickly. Nevertheless, it took precious time to tap a vein to the surface. 'OK, I'm in,' she said, attaching the line to the bag of saline. 'How's his BP doing?'

'Not good,' Brady murmured. 'He needs haemaccel, and fast.'

'Let's move it, then.'

'OK.' Brady shot upright. 'I'll bring the car round. The garden's pretty clear of shrubbery on this side. I should be able to reverse down beside the fence and we'll get Lester in without causing him too much added stress.'

Jo pulled her mobile from her back pocket. 'I'll call the hospital and let them know you're on the way in.' They both knew the elderly man's position could become critical very quickly if he didn't receive the benefit of a plasma expander.

'Will this do, Doctor?' Ellen was back, holding up a piece of sheeting.

'That's fine, Ellen.' Expertly, Jo folded the material into a manageable size to accommodate Lester's arm. Securing the sling gently, she tied the ends around his shoulder. 'Brady's just gone to bring his car round. Are you ready to go?'

Ellen nodded, her lips clamped tightly together. 'I've locked up and thrown a few things in a bag for Lester. They'll keep him in, won't they?'

'Yes, Ellen, they will.' Jo gave the older woman's shoulder a comforting little pat. 'They may operate tonight if they can get him stable enough. Otherwise it'll be first thing in the morning. But they really will look after him, so, please, don't fret.'

Ellen shook her greying head. 'You just never know, do you? Here we were planning a nice weekend—going to church and then the country markets—now all this…' She bit her lips together. 'My poor old Lester…'

Jo heart contracted. Ellen looked quite pale. And Jo guessed the adrenalin rush that had helped the elderly woman cope during the last few minutes had all but faded. She was exhibiting all the signs of post-trauma plus sheer mental exhaustion.

'Ellen, I'm just wondering…' Jo's look was concerned. 'Would you like me to give you something to help you over the shock of all this?'

'I'll be all right, thanks, dear.' Ellen lifted her chin, straightening the collar on her simple shirt-dress. 'A cup of tea will see me right. I'll get one at the hospital.'

Jo wasn't convinced. 'Well, if you're still feeling shaky later, just ask for someone to check you over—promise?'

Ellen nodded, determinedly hitching up her large

shoulder-bag as if steadying herself for this next phase of the journey.

'You and Lester were Dr Mitchell's patients, weren't you?' Jo asked, as the thought occurred to her. At Ellen's confirmation, she went on, 'Well, you'll automatically see Dr McNeal now—if that's what you want, of course.'

'Oh, yes. We'd be most happy to have Brady as our doctor. He's such a kind man, isn't he?'

Kind. The word stopped Jo in her tracks. The one and only attribute her mother insisted you simply *had* to witness in abundance in any man you were serious about.

Had she witnessed it in Brady? Jo's heart suddenly lurched into a mad scattering of beats. She had. Many times. Beginning right from when they'd first met and he'd offered to accompany her through that spooky car park. 'Yes, he is, Ellen,' she agreed, her voice a bit throaty. And then they looked up and saw Brady's taillights approaching as he carefully reversed down beside the fence towards them.

It was almost an hour and a half later when Brady got back from the hospital.

Jo went out on the front verandah to greet him as he left the car and began to make his way inside. 'Everything OK?' she asked.

'So far.' Brady rubbed a hand wearily across the back of his neck. 'I've spoken to the surgeon. He thinks they'll go for later tonight to do Lester.'

They walked into the lighted lounge. 'I encouraged Thea to go to her choir practice and told her I'd look after the bub,' Jo said. 'I hope that was all right?'

'Of course.' His mouth gave the merest twist of a smile. 'Is he asleep?'

'Right out of it. And I haven't started the meal. I thought I'd wait until you got home. You must be starved.'

'And you,' Brady observed. 'You didn't need to wait dinner for me, Jo. But thanks. I'll just throw myself under the shower.' He gave a dry grin. 'Get the smell of the hospital off me. But first I'll have a peep at AJ,' he added a bit sheepishly.

'I'll come with you.' Jo couldn't help herself. She couldn't get enough of Brady's baby boy.

They went along the hallway to the little bedroom he'd set aside as a nursery. 'I left the night-light on,' Jo whispered. 'Is that what you normally do?'

Brady nodded and they shared a moment of exquisite pleasure as they looked down at the sleeping infant.

'It's what it's all about, isn't it?' Brady caught her hand, and they left the nursery and began to retrace their steps along the hallway.

Suddenly he drew to a halt. 'Thank you so much for being here for AJ and me,' he said deeply.

'It's what friends do, isn't it?' she said, uneasily realising he was still holding her left hand and somehow, without her even knowing it, her other hand had crept up and was resting on his chest. What fabulous dark eyes he had, and his lashes—way too long for a man. And his son had inherited them. Another heartbreaker on his way to manhood...

'I'll, uh, get started with dinner, then,' she said jerkily, dragging her mind back to practical matters. Which was all a bit difficult when the most deliciously warm sensations seemed to be uncurling somewhere deep within her.

Ever so slightly, Brady tightened his fingers on hers. 'What a very odd evening we seem to be having.'

Was it her imagination—or did his voice sound deeper,

huskier? Jo licked her lips, saw his pupils dilate as his eyes followed the action. Was he going to kiss her? Did she want him to? She couldn't answer that. Quickly, almost as if her life depended on it, she lowered her gaze to blot out the all-male physical imprint.

Brady stayed very still, even though all that was male in him ached to draw her to him. To step outside the boundaries he'd set for himself, to really *touch* her. And, yes, to be touched in return.

The thought of something else far more urgent was enough to set the whole of him on fire.

In an abrupt movement he stepped away from her, roughly scrubbing a hand over his cheekbones. 'I'd better grab that shower.'

He *had* wanted to kiss her, Jo decided, tossing the onions, tomatoes and herbs together in a pan. Then why hadn't he? Surely she hadn't turned him off? Checking the water had come to the boil, she slid the spaghetti in and gave it a twirl.

Well, what now? She shrugged and gave a little huff of exasperation. Why was nothing between a man and a woman ever straightforward? But, then, wouldn't that all be just a bit dull and predictable?

With an impatient little '*tsk*' she began to grate the cheese to sprinkle over the finished pasta dish.

In the shower, Brady let the water pour over his head and shoulders and tried to untangle the strands of emotions that were tying his gut in knots.

Josephine. Jo.

He was captivated by everything about her. Her physicality for starters. And she was smart and savvy. So bright. So generous with everything she did. Generous?

He swore as he wrenched back the shower curtain and grabbed a towel. Was he going nuts? When before had he ever considered *generosity* as a necessary passport to any male-female relationship?

Hell. He was like a kid playing with fire. He flicked the zip closed on his jeans and dragged a white T-shirt over his head. He had to stop kidding himself. How could he let himself fall in love while Tanya's shadow was still hanging over him, enveloping him like some kind of restrictive overcoat?

The knife she'd shoved between his ribs was as sharp as the day she'd planted it there.

CHAPTER FIVE

'I SET the table out on the deck,' Jo said as Brady came back into the kitchen after his shower.

He blinked a bit and looked at her, and seemed to drag himself back from somewhere. 'Ah, good. Let's hope the mosquitoes don't eat us alive, then.'

Jo's mouth went up at the corners. 'Bit early for mozzies, actually.'

'Is it?' Brady watched as she scooped the tomato mixture from the pan and swirled it into the pasta. 'I must be a bit back to front with my seasons at the moment.'

Jo chuckled. 'What was it like, living in Canada?'

'It's a fabulous place, big-sky country like ours. And similar to Australia in terms of the vast distances we have to travel to get from place to place.'

'And you had a yen to go and explore somewhere different from your own country—was that it?' Jo assembled their food on a tray, adding forks and serviettes.

'Something like that.' Brady hefted the laden tray and led the way out onto the deck. 'In the beginning, it was Ben's idea.'

Jo's brows rose. 'Sophie's Ben?' She hadn't known that.

Brady nodded 'We were both in fairly predictable work

environments at the time and decided a change was called for. We negotiated a six-month exchange with two Canadian MOs from Winnipeg. After the six months were up, Ben returned to Australia. I decided to stay on and re-located to a rural practice in Alberta, near the foothills of the Rocky Mountains.'

'How fabulous,' she said wistfully. 'Lucky you.'

He flexed a shoulder. 'Nothing to stop you doing it.'

'S'pose not. I have travelled overseas a bit but not worked there—well, not yet anyway,' she qualified lightly.

Brady lifted the bottle of wine and refilled their glasses. 'I fell in love with the place,' he said quietly.

And with AJ's mother? Jo wondered silently. But Brady was now in full flow and she listened, entranced.

'I delved into the history of the Canadian Mounties while I was there. Found an excellent museum.'

'I've always been fascinated by the Mounties, too,' Jo admitted with a grin. 'They always look so spectacular on film.'

'Mmm. But these days their forces are quite diversified. They're deployed all over the world for various reasons, peace-keeping and so on.'

'What about their huskies?' Jo asked.

He laughed. 'Pensioned off, I should think. They've had to move with the times. Nowadays it's aircraft for many of their patrols. Sad really. But that's progress, as they say.'

Jo finished her wine and put the glass carefully back on the table. 'Compared with our long, hot summers here, I can imagine the sight of snow for so much of the year must have been different, to say the least. You must have experienced a white Christmas.'

He had and he went on to tell her about it at length.

'It would seem you made the most of every opportunity while you were there,' Jo said thoughtfully.

'It doesn't make much sense to live somewhere different and not come away richer for the experience.'

'No, I guess not. It would be a fine thing if we could all get out and travel, I suppose. We're so isolated here by our geographical position, aren't we?'

'We communicate with the rest of the world pretty well, though,' Brady said with an upside-down smile. 'Per capita, we're great users of information technology, according to what I hear.'

'Oh, technology…' Jo batted a hand in dismissal. 'It's so much more fun to experience a place for oneself or through the eyes of someone who's actually been there. Do you know, it might be a nice idea if you'd consider making a visit over to the primary school when you get a minute and organising a time to talk to the kids about Canada. Perhaps later on a bit, when it's getting close to Christmas. It would be such a treat for those little bush kids to have some hands-on information about another country, instead of peering at the net or looking at dry old maps.'

Brady looked startled. 'Would they welcome that, do you think?'

'Trust me.' Jo smiled. 'They certainly would. And I dare say the teachers would be grateful for a break in their normal routine.'

He hadn't meant to rabbit on like that. In one swift action Brady drained the last of his wine. Hell, he hadn't even told his parents half that stuff. Perhaps it was because Jo was so easy to talk to. That must be it. 'My time there did make a big impression on me,' he conceded quietly.

'Will you go back?' Jo's question was almost lost in the sound of the cicadas in the shrubbery adjacent to the deck.

He shrugged. 'Someday. I'll need to show AJ the country where he was born, I guess...'

And link up with his natural mother? The question popped into Jo's head but she didn't dare voice it. She could only hope that one day Brady would trust her enough to tell her his story. But it wouldn't be any time soon. Already she'd sensed the moment when he'd begun to withdraw back into himself in the slight tension that had stiffened his shoulders.

'The meal was wonderful, Jo—thanks,' he said, a bit gruffly. 'Got time for coffee?'

Jo glanced at her watch. It was nearly eleven o'clock. But it was Saturday tomorrow and neither of them had been rostered on call for the after-hours clinic. On the other hand... 'It's late. I should go. And you need all the sleep you can get.'

'You're probably right.' He shot her a rueful grin. 'I'll walk you out. No—leave all that,' he insisted, when she began to collect the dishes and put them back on the tray. 'I'll shove them in the dishwasher later.'

They walked outside to the front verandah. 'Oh— I did that map for Angelo's place,' Jo said. 'I left it on the coffee table in the lounge. I hope it's clear enough.'

'I'm sure it will be. Thanks. And thanks again for tonight. It was a great evening—at least for me.'

'And me,' Jo responded.

They'd moved close to the railings, looking out across the garden. Moonlight bathed the lawn in soft luminosity and a flurry of wind was stirring the leaves on the old mango tree into whispers.

'I should go,' Jo reiterated softly.

'I'll, uh, walk out to the car with you.'

'No need,' she said quickly. 'It's moonlight all the way. I'll be fine.'

'Jo…'

'Yes?'

'Nothing. I mean, just this…' He lifted a hand, his knuckles grazing her cheek softly, so softly, then down over the hollow of her throat until the backs of his fingers rested against the swell of her breast, just visible above the scooped neck of her top.

He gave a harshly indrawn breath and moved closer, turning his hand over so that his fingers lay against the rapidly beating pulse at the side of her throat.

'Brady… ' Jo's heart began pounding. In a tiny gesture of self-preservation she tried to turn away, but he gently caught her chin to bring her back and there was a long moment, a fluttering kind of sensation when anything was possible. Jo took a shaken breath, tilting her face up to his, thinking she should stop this now.

Before it was too late for both of them.

But Brady was already bending to her, his head descending slowly, inch by tormenting inch…

Just the thought of the physical act itself, the anticipation, made her feel wildly sensual, as if she wanted to go on tiptoe to meet him, take him to her, fuse his body with hers. And even in that split second while she thought about it, his lips had found their mark and claimed hers.

Jo sighed, absorbing the first touch of his mouth. First on her top lip, then her lower lip, with a touch so light, so delicate, like the brush of a butterfly's wing. Then his mouth firmed over hers, moving in a deep seductive rhythm, accentuating the tantalising taste of him, sending her senses into a heat wave of desire. And there was no part of her that felt untouched by the maleness of him in the heated passion of that one kiss.

She didn't want it to end. But, of course, it did. Perhaps good things, wild, pleasurable things, always did. And this one did with a mild oath from Brady, when the baby cried.

'He's determined to keep me in line,' he muttered ruefully, pressing his forehead against hers.

'Perfect timing.' Jo leaned back, her eyes flashing with light as she laughed softly. He looked into them just a little bit too long and suddenly they were marooned in uneasy silence.

'Ah, Jo…' His chest rose and fell in a long sigh. 'That wasn't supposed to happen.'

Jo swallowed, barely in control, and said the first thing that came into her head. 'But it has now, hasn't it?'

'Yes. And we can't take it back.'

'No.' Jo shivered when his thumb touched her full lower lip.

The baby cried insistently again and Brady turned towards the sound, torn.

'AJ needs you, Brady.'

'Yes.'

Slowly, Jo untwined his arms from where he'd looped them around her waist and took a decisive step backwards, away from him.

'I'll see you tomorrow,' he murmured, and then, as if still compelled to touch her, he reached for her, running his hands down her arms, lacing his fingers with hers.

'Go to your son,' Jo said softly, going on tiptoe to place

the softest kiss at the side of his mouth, before breaking his hold and almost running across the front lawn to the street. And the safety of her car.

Jo was a little late for the party but there was plenty of parking space on the big acre block when she arrived at the Kouras residence the following evening. She'd been delayed by a phone call from Fliss just as she'd been about to leave.

Recalling the conversation, her mouth twitched in a wry smile. Fliss had been full of it, of course, shrieking in disbelief when Jo had relayed the amazing coincidence of Brady turning up to work at the Mt Pryde practice.

'So how far have you got with him?' Fliss had come straight to the point.

'Don't start fishing,' Jo had replied, 'because I'm not biting.'

'Ah!' Fliss decided she'd hit gold. 'Told you he was worth a second look—and he's eligible.'

Jo snorted. 'Your famous grapevine didn't mention Brady is a single dad, did it?'

'He's *what*?'

'He has a six-month-old son.'

'And you're nuts about kids,' Fliss's response rippled with speculation. 'Hey, this could really work!'

Jo felt her skin warm and changed tack quickly. 'How's the delicious Daniel?'

'Oh, you know,' Fliss sighed. 'Being a pilot. Here today and gone tomorrow.'

Jo laughed. 'Do you good to stay home occasionally.'

'And I am, you know.' Fliss sounded a bit glum.

'Saturday night and I'm being a good little girl while Dan hops across to Auckland for the weekend.'

'I've no doubt you'll survive. But, unlike you, I do have a party to go to. I was just about out the door.'

'Party for two, is it?'

'It's a practice do,' Jo said patiently. 'Our senior partner's leaving.'

'But Brady will be there, right?'

Jo groaned. 'He's a member of the practice so of course he'll be there.'

'Well, have fun. And keep me posted.'

Jo got out of the car and took a deep satisfying breath of cool night air that was laced with the pungency of eucalyptus trees. Angelo and his wife Penny Chou—she continued to use her maiden name—lived high on a hill in an old Queenslander-style home they had faithfully and lovingly restored to its former glory.

They were so lucky to live here, Jo thought, looking upwards to where the stars were splashed across the night sky, as though a giant hand had thrown a fistful of diamonds into all that space.

As she began making her way towards the house, she thought of Angelo and Penny themselves. They were devoted and had recently celebrated their tenth wedding anniversary. Jo sometimes wondered whether they intended having children. If so, they were leaving it a bit late. Perhaps they didn't feel the need—there was that, of course.

She herself wanted a brood of kids, Jo decided, suddenly feeling an odd kind of urgency about it. Well, perhaps not a brood—three, perhaps. Even a fourth, if one came along.

She smiled at the thought of what would be considered

a large family in today's society. But they'd have such fun. She imagined little girls in big shady hats helping her tend the flower garden and sturdy boys who would want bikes and play football and have dark eyes and melting smiles like their father...

Their *father*. Oh, lord. A long slow quiver ran down her backbone at the fantasy.

For heaven's sake, get a grip, she berated herself silently. Nevertheless her pulse began racing when she remembered Brady's kiss, remembered the feel of his mouth on hers, the sensation of his body against her own, the touch of his hands on her skin.

And she wanted it to happen again, wanted to feel those same sensations again.

Her pulse began racing. Within a couple of minutes she'd be seeing him, perhaps standing next to him. At the thought her heart thudded against her ribs and she drew a steadying breath before stepping into the lighted space and the wonderfully atmospheric outdoor area Angelo and Penny had created for entertaining their guests.

Everyone had arrived, by the look of things. Jo's eyes scanned the assembled company, seeing Lilian in a little circle with Monica and Marika and Marika's two little girls, while their respective husbands stood at the barbecue with Angelo, beers in hand and all obviously enjoying the male camaraderie. So why wasn't Brady among them?

Jo couldn't account for the sudden sense of disappointment she felt. She hesitated and wondered if perhaps he was upstairs, settling the baby. Yes, of course. That's where she'd find him.

Ducking behind a lattice screen, she took the back stairs to the verandah, encountering Tom and his latest girlfriend, Ashlee, along with Vicki and Jared, all making their way back down. Jo smiled. Penny obviously had them working.

She fluttered a wave, returning their casual greetings, watching them laugh and joke as they juggled the laden trays. She heard Tom grumbling he was starved and shook her head. They all seemed so—so *young*. So happy, so free of responsibility.

'Jo! Hi, sweetie!' Penny turned from placing something in the fridge as Jo walked into the kitchen. 'Have you just arrived?'

'Sorry, I'm a bit late,' Jo apologised. 'Can I help with anything?' *And is Brady here?*

Penny shook her head, her inky-black hair rippling across her shoulders. 'I'm all sorted, thanks. Like to see what I've done for dessert?' She sent Jo a hopeful look. 'Hope everyone likes pears.'

'Oh, I'm sure they do,' Jo responded. 'Pears are gorgeous and right in season just now.'

'Mmm. Angelo's dad sent us a couple of cases, so I'm feeling bound to use them wherever I can.' She removed the covering from the cake stand. 'I've made an upside-down pear and chocolate cake. This recipe serves twelve so that should be enough to go around.'

Jo made a small moue. 'If Tom doesn't come back for seconds.'

'I never thought of that,' Penny said, her face deadpan. 'Oh, dear.'

For a second there was silence and then they lost the battle and laughed. And laughed.

'We shouldn't be mean about Tom.' Jo took a steadying breath and looked suitably chastened. 'And the cake looks fabulous, Pen. But you should have let me bring something.'

'Don't be silly. You know Angelo and I love to cook. Now, along with the cake, I've done poached pears and some ginger shortbread to go with them.'

'My mouth's watering already.'

Penny gave a chuckle. 'Well, you'll have to get through a steak and a mountain of salads first.' She swept a few things into the dishwasher and closed the door. 'I'm hoping we can make it a nice evening for Ralph and Lilian. Be good if they could unwind and relax—at least for a couple of hours.'

'It's so sad they're leaving under these circumstances,' Jo agreed.

'It may have a happy ending yet,' Penny said. 'I've spoken at length to Dominic Carroll, the oncologist treating their grandson. He's actually a friend from my time as a resident at St Vincent's in Sydney. According to Dom, Michael's last lot of blood tests were very encouraging.'

'That news must have given Ralph and Lilian a huge lift.'

Penny nodded. 'Somewhat. But I guess with cancer one never really feels out of the woods, do they? And the stress for the family is horrendous.'

'The very reason why Ralph and Lilian are keen to share the load and be of some support to their son and his wife.'

'Oh, lord—enough shop talk.' Penny turned and touched Jo on the arm. 'Everything's under control here so let's join the others, shall we?'

'Good idea.' *Perhaps Brady will have arrived by now.*

'Tom's girl seems nice,' Penny remarked, as they made their way down the stairs.

'I've spoken to her a couple of times at the surgery when she came to see Tom. Yes, she does seem nice. Pretty, too.'

'And young,' Penny groaned.

'Does she have a job, do you know?'

'University, I believe. Secondary teaching, majoring in drama.'

Against the twinkling mischief in Penny's eyes, Jo kept a straight face with difficulty. 'I didn't say a word.'

When they rejoined the party, Penny went off to circulate while Jo again looked in vain for Brady's distinctive dark head among the guests. Again she was disappointed.

'Uh—Dr Rutherford?'

Jo spun round. 'Oh—hi, Chris.' She acknowledged Monica's young teenage son, who was helping out with the drinks. 'Thanks.' Almost absently, she reached out and took a glass of white wine from the tray he was shyly proffering.

She took a mouthful of the crisp Riesling and then, stopping for a brief word here and there, she purposefully made her way across to Angelo, who was still at his post at the barbecue. Once there, she sniffed appreciatively. 'The steaks smell wonderful.'

'That's the special marinade,' Angelo said with some pride. 'I've made up some kebabs as well. The youngsters seem to like them. And the butcher threw in some gourmet sausages as his contribution.'

'Good grief,' Jo said weakly. 'We'll be eating all night.'

Angelo grinned and swallowed a mouthful of his lager. 'Don't you believe it. This lot will go nowhere once the guys line up for a feed.'

'Talking of the guys,' Jo said, with a faintly strained smile, 'I don't see Brady here.'

'Rang earlier. AJ's spiked a bit of a temp. Brady thought he'd err on the side of caution and stay home with him. Pity. I know he was looking forward to being here this evening.'

Jo bit her lip. Well, she'd thought so, too. And why hadn't he let *her* know? 'I've taken AJ on to my list. Perhaps I should pop over and just check on him.'

'Ah.' Angelo quickly bent back to the barbecue and deftly began turning the steaks. 'Brady thought you'd feel like that, Jo. He said for you to enjoy the party and not to worry. He'll call if he needs you.'

If he needs you.

There wasn't much comfort in the words, Jo decided. And why *hadn't* he called her? It would have seemed the logical thing to do, instead of sending a message via Angelo. Well, obviously he hadn't wanted to talk to her.

Now she was forced to wonder whether in the cold light of day he'd decided the intimate moments they'd shared had been a very bad idea. But he'd been the one to initiate that kiss. Her thoughts flew in wild conjecture. Perhaps the baby wasn't unwell at all? Perhaps Brady had invented the whole thing simply to steer clear of her? At least outside working hours. That sounded nearer the truth.

Well, damn him, Jo thought in swift fury. Turning away convulsively, she made her way over to where Ralph and Lilian were sitting. At least she'd be sure of a welcome there.

It was after midnight when Jo got home. She and Monica had stayed longer than the others to help Penny with the last of the clearing-up.

And despite the reasons for holding it, the party had been lovely. Amongst such love and goodwill from friends and colleagues, Ralph and Lilian had obviously found themselves able to relax and enjoy themselves.

The staff at the practice had presented them with a painting by a local artist. It was a glorious water-colour featuring the countryside around Mt Pryde, where Ralph and Lilian had spent so many happy years.

And then Angelo, who loved a bit of ceremony, had cleared his throat and presented Ralph with a very impressive-looking parchment envelope, along with a little speech.

'This is from all of us at the surgery, mate. Passport to a luxury weekend at the Gold Coast, with every bit of pampering thrown in. So, when you feel like giving yourselves a treat, we hope you and Lilian will take advantage of it and enjoy every second.'

Ralph had been visibly touched, Lilian teary, her face crumpling as she'd thanked everyone. 'This gift is so very thoughtful,' she'd said. 'Little Michael's illness has brought home to us the value of real friendship, the kind of friendship we've found here at Mt Pryde. And Ralph has promised me we'll be back for visits from time to time.'

'You can bet on that,' Ralph had chimed in, adding his thanks to Lilian's. 'And I'd like it known that I intend to keep myself up to date with what's going on in medicine so any time the practice needs a locum, please, don't hesitate to call on me.'

'You beauty!' Tom had whooped. 'Feel free to put in your holiday requests on Monday, guys. We've got us a locum.'

That statement had brought laughter and applause, as it had been meant to. And diffused the slight tension that everyone's overloaded emotions had suddenly brought to the surface.

Brady should have been there to experience it all, Jo

thought thinly. She knew Ralph had prepared a little speech of welcome for him—a few chosen words that would have made Brady feel an integral part of the practice now Ralph was officially going.

Well, he'd missed the opportunity for that to happen and she knew Ralph had had the feeling of things being slightly unfinished.

In a weary gesture Jo raised her arms and stretched, dragging her fingers through her hair and shaking it out. Despite his rather blunt message to the contrary, she *would* call Brady tomorrow—or today as it was now.

He couldn't dodge her for ever. And in Jo's opinion, whether he liked it or not, Dr Brady McNeal had some explaining to do.

CHAPTER SIX

JO WOKE late and with a headache. Her head had been fuzzy from when it had touched the pillow. And it wasn't from the effects of too much wine, she thought bitterly. The reason she hadn't been able to coax sleep was because of all this business with Brady.

Sighing, she threw back the covers and made her way to the shower.

Later, dressed in a pair of cotton trousers and a loose white shirt, she sat over a cup of tea and some toast spread with honey and tried to think about a plan of action.

Somehow, she'd gone off the idea of calling him. Telephone conversations tended to be a bit impersonal and certain nuances in voice patterns interpreted wrongly. It was so much easier when you were face to face with someone. Then you had body language to guide you.

That's what I'll do, she decided. I'll go over to his house and speak to him personally. That way I'll know if he's feeling awkward about what's happened between us. And if he is? a little voice said.

Jo lifted a shoulder dismissively. Surely they'd be able to talk about it—wouldn't they? She quickly got to her feet. Perhaps she should go now, before she lost all her courage.

As she neared Brady's house, Jo slowed her car to a crawl. The nerves in her stomach felt tied in knots. It would be so easy to drive straight past and simply return home. But that wouldn't solve anything and she'd be left wondering for the rest of the day.

Pulling up on the opposite side of the road, she cut the engine and wondered what Brady's reaction would be when he saw her. As she leant forward to remove the key from the ignition, she raised her head and looked across at his cottage. And frowned uncertainly.

A dark blue sedan was blocking his driveway. The car was unfamiliar to Jo. It was no one from the practice, she decided. Obviously he had visitors from out of town.

Well, that put paid to her own plans. There was no way she could intrude on his Sunday now.

She felt a sense of frustration, mixed with hurt and disappointment, as she restarted the car and took off. Her talk with Brady would have to wait until she saw him at the surgery tomorrow.

Jo was full of misgivings as she drove to work on Monday. Most of her anger with Brady had faded. Now she just wanted to find out where they stood—if they stood anywhere at all. But whatever, something had to be done to clear the air or their situation at work would become awkward and in the end untenable.

As she drove into her parking space at the rear of the surgery, Jo glanced over the vehicles already there and frowned a bit. Everyone, including Brady, seemed to have arrived. Jo glanced at her watch. She wasn't late.

Collecting her case from the passenger seat, she got out of the car and locked the door. Perhaps they'd all had the same idea of wanting to get to work early to make sure the practice didn't start falling apart from day one, now that Ralph was officially gone.

As usual, Jo stopped off in her room to deposit her medical case and then went along to the staffroom. She pushed open the door, finding only Angelo, Tom and Vicki there and the usual air of cheerfulness missing. Jo got her coffee and offered a tentative smile around the room. 'Nice party, wasn't it?'

'Yes,' Angelo, now the senior partner, said economically. 'Ralph and Lilian left this morning, by the way.'

'Ralph was always so nice to me,' Vicki sighed, a little catch in her voice. 'Even when I stuffed up appointments now and again. He never went ballistic. I'm so-o going to miss him.'

'For crying out loud, Vic,' Tom growled. 'Get over it! We're *all* going to miss Ralph.' Peeling himself away from the wall, he stalked out.

'Oh, pathetic!' Vicki said stormily. 'And he didn't wash his coffee-mug!'

Angelo rolled his eyes, linking Jo in a long-suffering look. He said quietly, 'I'd like to try for a lunchtime meeting today, if you can manage it, please? Just to bed things down a bit.'

'Should be fine.' Jo nodded.

'Good. Brady thinks he can make it as well.'

'He's in, then?' Of course he was in. She'd seen his car.

'In his room. Some paperwork to catch up on, he said.'

'Oh, OK. I'll just pop in on him and see how his weekend went,' she fibbed. Leaving her barely touched coffee, she fled the room.

Outside Brady's consulting room, Jo took a deep breath

and knocked. Hearing his gruff 'Yes?' she put a hand over her thumping heart and went in.

'Hi.' She forced a tentative smile. 'Do you have a minute?'

'Jo.' He looked surprised.

Jo saw him quickly school his expression, but not before she'd read his body language. He was obviously brooding about something, she decided, his thoughts somewhere else…or with someone else.

'Have a seat,' he offered, scooting his own chair back from the desk and folding his arms across his chest. Waiting.

'Thanks.' Jo felt disorientated. She'd been in this office countless times when it had been Ralph's domain but this morning, for some reason, it felt like alien territory. She licked her lips. 'Am I disturbing you?'

Brady merely lifted a shoulder in response. 'What's up?'

'I just wondered how AJ was.'

'He's fine now, thanks. It was just one those infant things.'

'I wouldn't have minded calling in and checking him over, you know.'

Once the words were out, Jo wished she could have re-phrased them. They'd sounded like an accusation of some kind and it was obvious Brady thought so as well. A tiny muscle tightened beside his mouth. 'I'm a doctor, Jo. I *do* know what to look for.'

Nettled by his glib answer, she asked thinly, 'Why didn't you let me know you couldn't make the party?'

'I wasn't aware I had to. Angelo was the host. I called him and made my apologies.'

So, end of story apparently. Jo stood abruptly and put her hands across the back of the chair. 'In that case, I'm sorry I worried about you.' She gave a humourless little laugh. 'Silly me…'

'Jo—wait!' A look that was something like pain crossed his face and he spun off his chair and came to stand beside her. 'I've upset you, and I'm sorry,' he said, his voice tight.

Jo turned and brought her head up, frowning uncertainly. 'You look tired.'

He lifted a hand and rubbed the back of his neck. 'It's been a hell of a weekend.'

'Because of the baby?'

'I was up and down to him a fair bit.'

Her throat constricted at the whole scenario his words had evoked. 'I would've helped, Brady.'

He shook his head. 'It's not your responsibility, Jo. It's mine. But, providentially, my folks arrived unexpectedly on Sunday. Mum took over and I managed some sleep in the afternoon. But she has a very demanding job so I can't expect her to make the trip too often.'

That explained the unfamiliar car. Jo bit the corner of her lip. 'Do you feel able to work? If not, we can cover—'

'Of course I'm fit to work,' he broke in tersely. 'It was a bit of a glitch that's all. For crying out loud, don't go imagining I'll turn out to be some kind of lame duck in the practice.'

No, Jo fumed silently, just a prickly and too-damned-independent-for-your-own-good one. 'Look, Brady,' she said, her voice not quite steady, 'Ralph always insisted that as a team we supported one another, both professionally and personally. And when he gave his farewell speech on Saturday night, he said he hoped that would continue. Am I making myself clear?'

'Perfectly,' he drawled, in the same dismissive tone he'd used earlier. 'Lecture heard and understood. Now, you hear me. *I can manage fine.*'

'I hope so,' she retorted, colour warming her cheeks. 'And next time you're at the pharmacy, get something for your stiff-necked pride!'

It was surprising how much it hurt to be off-side with him.

Jo went back to her room and shut the door quietly, feeling a sad kind of disappointment close in on her. She thought, Well, that's that.

She and Brady had shared a kiss, a brief passionate interlude. And it was a big jump from there to a relationship. Yet she hadn't imagined the almost tangible physical pull between them. She *hadn't*. The vibe had been there, singing and throbbing like the strings of a cello.

But now it seemed obvious that Brady was setting down new ground rules, leaving her out of any discussion on the matter. In fact, he'd been cutting when all she'd done had been to care about him and his baby…

Sliding into her chair, she switched on her computer, the morning's long patient list oddly coming as a relief from her unhappy thoughts.

Halfway through the morning, Vicki knocked on Jo's door and came in. 'I have Stacey Owens on the phone. She knows it's short notice but she'd really appreciate a chat about young Lachlan. He's gone ratty again. Driving her and Paul up the wall.'

Jo felt a wave of sympathy for the farming family who had had their little boy back and forth to hospital for the whole of his young life. 'He's due for another operation soon. Now and again it all gets too much for him. So, yes, tell Stacey it's fine. Just pop her in at the end of this morning's list, thanks, Vic.'

It would mean she would probably only get to the tail end

of the staff meeting, Jo thought ruefully, but her patients' welfare came first. Besides, it would give her a legitimate excuse not to cross Brady's path again until she had to.

In the few minutes she had free before Stacey's appointment, Jo used the time to get Lachlan's details up on the computer and bring herself up to date.

Such a long road it had been for the little boy, she thought, speed-reading Lachlan's history. He'd been born with the rare Moebius syndrome, a condition that prevented him from using the muscles in his face. So at age six, Lachlan hadn't yet been able to smile.

The path for the reconstructive surgery was of necessity slow and tedious, but after this upcoming operation Joshua Faraday, Lachlan's specialist surgeon in Sydney, was hopeful of some dramatic improvement.

Jo decided she needed more information at her disposal for when Stacey arrived. The logical course would be to contact Josh Faraday. He was a personal friend, calm and compassionate and somewhat of a ground-breaker in this kind of surgery, and Jo knew he would be sympathetic to the parents' state of mind. Without thinking further, she buzzed Vicki.

'Stacey hasn't arrived yet, Jo,' Vicki said apologetically.

'That's OK. Would you try to get Dr Faraday at St Cecelia's in Sydney for me, please, Vic? If he's in surgery, just leave a message that I'd appreciate a call from him, as soon as he can manage it.'

Only a few moments later Vicki was back on the line. 'I have Dr Faraday for you, Jo.'

'Thanks. Josh, hi! It's Jo Rutherford.'

'How's tricks, Jo?' The surgeon's relaxed greeting came down the line.

'Good. How's married life?'

He gave a soft chuckle. 'Stunning. You should try it.'

'Chance would be a fine thing.'

He snorted. 'What's wrong with the males up there? Are they blocks of wood from the feet up?'

Jo's mouth curled on a hard-edged laugh. 'Some of them for sure…' Her gaze snapped up as a rap sounded on her door and Brady poked his head in. Her heart missed a beat and she lost her train of thought for a second.

'I'll come back,' he mouthed.

Jo shook her head and beckoned him in. She pointed him to a chair and resumed her phone conversation. 'Josh, I wanted to speak to you about a Moebius syndrome patient, young Lachlan Owens.'

'I'm operating on him next week,' the surgeon said. 'Coincidentially, we've just finished a team meeting about the procedure we'll use for this one. It's his twelfth, by the way.'

'That's why I'm calling, actually. I'm about to have a chat to his mother, Stacey,' Jo explained. 'Lachlan is fretting again about having to go back to hospital, giving her and his dad a hard time. I wonder—could you clue me in a bit about the actual surgery you'll be doing this time and the results you expect? Then I'll have something concrete to pass on to her and maybe between us we can help her allay Lachlan's fears.'

'Well, first off, it's essential she tries to keep Lachlan optimistic,' Josh emphasised. 'I realise he's only a little lad, but he's quick. These are some points you could make to her, Jo.'

Jo listened, making quick notes on the pad beside her. Finally, she said, 'Thanks so much, Josh. This information should go a long way towards giving the parents some sense of optimism about Lachlan's future. I just hope I can interpret it without making too many bloopers.'

'Jo,' he said kindly, 'if all my referring GPs were as clued in as you, I'd be out of a job.'

'Impossible!' Jo chuckled. 'But nice to hear. Give my best to Alex.'

'Shall do. Bye, now.'

'Bye, Josh. Thanks, again.' Jo replaced the receiver carefully and brought her head up, looking directly at Brady. 'Can I help you with something?'

He returned her gaze unflinchingly. 'I'll get straight to the point. I came to apologise for this morning's debacle. I'm an idiot and I need my butt kicked.'

Jo hardened her heart. If he thought he could pick her up and put her down whenever he felt like it, he had another think coming. 'Tell someone who cares, Brady.'

He frowned uncertainly and a smear of colour reddened his throat, before he said, 'I really value your...*friendship*, Jo. I want you to know that.'

Well, good for you, Jo thought sourly, and for a few moments they sat in awkward silence. 'If you want me to be Andrew's doctor, you have to let me treat him,' she pointed out quietly. 'I could have put your mind at rest, if nothing else.'

'I know. I wanted to call you but I held back.'

'Why?'

His hand tightened around the paperweight on her desk and he lowered his gaze. 'You're a very caring person. Probably too caring for your own good.' He swallowed as though something was jamming his throat. 'My personal life at the moment is hardly uncomplicated. I...would hate to lead you into something that might leave you hurt—in any way.'

Jo rode out his little rider with a small lift of her shoulders. 'That's rather admitting defeat before we've even begun to know each other. We deserve better than that, don't you think?'

Brady didn't know what to think any more. He was stuffed to the gills with *thinking*. He heaved a sigh. Perhaps it *was* time to slough off the log of wood he'd been carrying on his shoulder for what seemed like ages. There were plenty of sole parents in the same boat—mostly women, he admitted. But from what he'd observed, they just got on with their lives. They certainly didn't go around looking for twenty-foot holes to fall into. Metaphorically, of course. Just the thought brought a grim smile to his lips. He glanced across at Jo with something like a plea for under-standing in his eyes. 'I really would like the chance for us to get to know each other—if that's all right?'

Jo was cautious. 'If you're going to blow hot and cold, Brady, it's not all right.'

'No,' he agreed, his look steady. Should he tell her now about Tanya? he agonised. How she'd dumped him, dumped him and AJ both. But then Jo would probably think he was going for the sympathy vote. And he didn't want that. 'Emo-tionally, I'm treading water a bit,' he said instead.

Jo's heart gave a sideways skip. 'That's understandable. Something tells me you still have unfinished business with AJ's mother,' she said bravely.

His mouth moved in a bitter travesty of a smile. 'That's where you're wrong, Jo. My business with AJ's mother is quite, quite finished. She doesn't want either of us. Ever. So, what am I supposed to tell my son?'

She held his gaze for a long heartbeat, feeling a surge of empathy with him, then said cautiously, 'Perhaps, from now on, you need to live your own life and leave those kinds of decisions until later.'

He seemed to give it some thought. 'Maybe I could try, at least. My mother told me to lighten up,' he added, a bit sheepishly.

Jo smiled. 'I like the sound of your mother.' She glanced at her watch. 'I don't want to rush you, Brady, but I've a patient due. Well, a patient's mum in this case. She must be running late.'

Brady's attention was immediately engaged and it was as though they'd never had those awkward moments only seconds ago. He leaned forward, pressing both hands on the desktop in front of him. 'I couldn't help overhearing your conversation. It reminded me of a patient I inherited while I was practising in Canada, a little guy called Willard North. He had the same syndrome. So I do know something about it.'

'How extraordinary! Moebius is pretty rare. How old was your little fellow?'

'From memory, around six. He came on to my list towards the end of his treatment and then I followed him through the final two operations. I actually stayed in touch with the family afterwards.'

'So the surgery worked, then?'

'Beautifully. What's the next step for your little guy?'

'A muscle transplant.'

Brady nodded. 'That's mostly the way they do it, from what I've seen. And this is the op that will give him the ability to smile, is that it?'

'Hopefully, yes. That's what his surgeon is aiming for.'

'So it's a good-news story. And it will happen, Jo. I've seen it with my own eyes.'

Jo made a swift decision. 'Are you desperate for your lunch, Brady?'

His head went back and he looked a bit puzzled. 'Not really—why?'

'I wondered if you'd sit in on my consultation with Stacey. The family have been to hell and back with hospitals and doctors since Lachlan was born. I think they're possibly still a bit sceptical about the results of yet another operation, despite what the surgeon says. If you could tell Stacey about your own experience with Moebius…? '

'I'd be happy to,' he said slowly. 'If you're sure I won't be sticking my oar in.'

Jo waved away his misgivings. 'Believe me, Stacey will welcome any information you can give her. Now, I'd better buzz Angelo and tell him we'll both be a bit late for the staff meeting.'

'It's OK.' Brady swung up quickly. 'I'll go and see him. Few fences to mend there as well,' he said ruefully.

'The air was as thick as porridge when I walked in this morning,' Jo said. 'You didn't have words, did you?'

'Nothing like that,' he dismissed. 'The place was like a wake when I arrived. I'm afraid I was a bit short with everyone.' His lips moved in a rueful twist. 'Ralph's departure has obviously left a big personal gap.'

And Brady was under the impression they expected *him* to fill it? Jo was stunned. If that's what he'd interpreted from any of their actions or words, no wonder he was feeling a bit off-side. But he couldn't have been more wrong. Still, on the other hand, perhaps they'd all rattled on a bit much about Ralph and how he'd be missed.

'You're not here to fill a *gap* of any kind, Brady. And if that's the impression we've given you, I can only say I'm sorry. You're here on your own merits, for heaven's sake! And speaking personally, I haven't seen anything that tells me you're not an excellent doctor and the right choice for this practice.'

'Thanks,' he murmured, and it sounded like a caress. 'Feels good to have you on my side, Dr Rutherford.'

He left the room and was back a few minutes later.

Jo looked up from her computer screen. 'All sorted?'

'Yep.' Brady slid into his chair once more. 'Angelo's no fool. He'd come to his own conclusion about things. He's cancelled today's meeting. Instead, we'll get back to normal and have our usual weekly meeting on Fridays.'

'Thank goodness for that,' Jo said with relief.

'Sorry, I couldn't get here any sooner...' Stacey Owens was full of apologies when she finally made it into Jo's consulting room. 'The school rang just as I was about to leave. Lachlan was playing up a treat. They asked me to come and collect him. Vicki's offered to look after him for a bit,' she rushed on. 'I hope that's all right.'

'Stacey, it's perfectly fine,' Jo hastened to reassure the young mother. 'Vicki's a natural with children. This is Dr McNeal,' Jo introduced Brady. 'I've asked him to sit in with us because he has some knowledge of Moebius.'

'It's all getting to Paul and me a bit,' Stacey admitted, biting down on her bottom lip. 'We've delayed having another child because of the time and energy we've had to devote to Lachlan...'

'But Dr Rutherford tells me you're nearing the end of the road, as far as his treatment is concerned,' Brady came in professionally.

Stacy gave a helpless little shrug. 'I'm not sure what the surgeons are going to do this time.'

'I've just spoken to Dr Faraday, Stacey,' Jo said.

'They're going to be transplanting a muscle from Lachlan's inner leg to his face. After the operation, things will take time to settle down, of course, and Lachlan will need some further work with a speech therapist. But this operation is the one that will allow your little boy to smile.'

Stacey looked unconvinced and Brady said bracingly, 'I've seen it happen, Stacey. Lachlan will be like any other child after the implant of the new muscle. Then it will be one positive thing after another until you'll all be taking his brand-new smile for granted.'

'Dr Faraday told us there'll still be another operation after this one.' Stacey bowed her head and looked at her hands. 'I honestly don't know if we'll be able to get Lachlan back to the hospital again. He's really cracked up this time as it is.'

'The final operation will be to fix the other side of his face.' Brady leaned over to grab Jo's scribble pad and began to draw a diagram, quickly sketching the outline of a child's face. 'At the moment, I imagine Lachlan's face looks something like this, right?'

Stacey nodded.

'And the main reason for him being unable to smile is because he has no biting-down reflex.' With swift strokes, Brady illustrated what he meant. 'How about putting yourself in the same boat?' Brady's quirked brows shot the challenge to the young mother.

'You mean pretend I'm Lachlan?' Stacey looked taken aback but nevertheless tried the experiment and succeeded in making only a grimace.

'It's not easy, is it?' Brady commiserated gently.

'No.' Stacey raised questioning eyes. 'I don't think I've really understood that before. And that's the reason my son can't smile?'

'Basically, yes.' Brady flicked a quick look across to Jo and gave her an almost imperceptible nod.

Jo came in on cue. 'But according to Dr Faraday, this next operation will go a long way towards improving Lachlan's speech and the way he moves his mouth,' she said encouragingly.

'It's a win-win situation,' Brady added. 'You'll find Lachlan's sense of self-worth will go up dramatically, and school, instead of being the place where he feels uncomfortable, will suddenly become fun.'

Stacey raised her head from the drawing, linking both doctors with a strained smile. 'Thanks for explaining it. Dr Faraday has as well, but it's hard to take everything in when you're already stressed and having to cope all over again.'

'And away from home,' Jo sympathised. 'Is Paul going with you this time?'

The young mother shook her head. 'He has to be here for the pickers. Several of the crops will be ready for harvesting. But I'll be OK,' she said bravely. 'There's a little B&B where I stay. The rates are reasonable and it's near the hospital so I can spend most of the time with Lachlan.' She bit her lip and asked Jo tentatively, 'Did Dr Faraday say how long the surgery will take this time?'

'He expects it to take five to seven hours. It's an extremely delicate procedure. But Dr Faraday is very skilled. He won't want to skimp on anything that will lessen your little boy's chance of a perfect result.'

'I hardly dare think he might be *normal* one day.' Stacey gave a cracked laugh and scrubbed a couple of stray tears from her cheeks.

'He will be.' Jo put a comforting hand on the young mother's shoulder and squeezed. 'But enough now,' she

cajoled lightly. 'I'm sure you want to get home to your husband.'

Stacey nodded, looking embarrassed. 'This has been
really great of you—thank you both.'

'That's what we're here for,' Jo said. 'Come on, now. I'll
walk you out and we'll collect Lachlan from Vicki.'

When Jo returned to her office, Brady was still there,
parked against the window-frame, looking out. Jo had to
call him twice before he registered. 'You OK?' she asked.

'Just thinking.' His mouth compressed for a moment.
'And I've thought of a way we could help Stacey and her
family.'

Jo moved across to the cooler and got herself a glass of
water. 'I imagined that's what we'd just been doing.'

Brady flicked a hand in rebuttal. 'They need more than
doctors spouting medical lingo. What they do need is some
kind of tangible proof that this surgery can work. I'm going
to contact Abe and Ginny North in Canada. I know they
kept pictures of Will's face before and after he'd had the
surgery. The last one showed him with a full-blown smile.
I'll ask them to send me some copies.'

'Would they mind?'

'Not when they know what it's for. And if they email
them to me this week, we could have the printouts to show
the Owens by the weekend.'

'Sounds workable.' Jo's eyes widened and she smiled.
'Then we could take a run out to the Owenses' farm so
Stacey and Paul could have a good browse through them.
Lachlan as well. Oh, Brady, thank you for offering to do this.'

He shrugged her thanks away. 'It's just walking a mile
in someone's else's shoes, Jo. I can only imagine what it's
been like for Stacey and her husband.'

'Yes…' Jo's teeth bit softly into her lower lip. Just as *she* could only imagine what it was like for Brady to have the sole care and responsibility of his infant son day in, day out and stretching on into an unknown kind of future…

CHAPTER SEVEN

'So, THAT'S what Brady and I have come up with,' Jo con-
cluded. It was near the end of the Friday staff meeting and
she looked hopefully between Angelo and Tom.

'Sounds very proactive.' Tom was enthusiastic, looking
at the computer printouts Brady had brought in. 'And these
are of your little Moebius guy from Canada, Brady?'

Brady nodded. 'That's Will. His mum included a recent
shot of him as well. Looks like a regular kid these days,
doesn't he?'

'I must say, this is rural medicine at its best,' Angelo said
approvingly. 'Well done, both of you.'

Jo smiled, giving Brady a quick glance from under her
eyelids. 'We've arranged to go out to the Owenses' place
tomorrow afternoon. They're pretty keen to see the photos.
And it'll be a chance for Brady to have a look at the countryside as well.'

'Good, good.' Angelo nodded approvingly. 'Excellent.
Then, perhaps—' He began to add something more but
closed his mouth abruptly.

Seeing the action, Jo gave him a mental tick of approval.
She guessed Angelo had at last realised that they all had to
stop trying to 'sell' the place to Brady. He'd signed a

contract for a year. Whether he was happy with Mt Pryde, the practice and his colleagues after that period, only time would tell.

The meeting began to break up quickly. 'I'm on call at the after-hours clinic,' Angelo informed the others. 'But I'll be on my mobile if anyone needs me for anything.' He made for the door. 'Have a good weekend, all.'

'You, too,' they chorused and began to shuffle their paperwork together and make a general exodus.

Weather-wise, it was a lovely afternoon. And Jo said as much to Brady when he arrived to collect her. With the baby already asleep in his capsule in the back seat and the peace of the countryside settling over them, they drove towards the Owenses' farm.

'You obviously know Stacey and Paul pretty well,' Brady said.

'Mmm.' Jo nodded. 'They were both born and bred here. Got married very young. Stacey was twenty, I think, and Paul a year older.'

'Lord, I can't imagine that.' Brady shook his head. 'Still, they must be a strong unit if they're still together through all of Lachlan's problems. Takes grit to do that. In my experience, too many guys do a runner and leave their partners to cope when things get tough.'

Jo stayed silent and let the words sink in, and wondered whether that's what had happened in Brady's past relationship. Except in his case it had obviously been AJ's mother who had done the running.

'The Owenses' house is just up here, past that belt of trees,' Jo said, later, as they drove up a winding dirt track, past a couple of round-bellied ponies and several inquisitive grey wallabies, who'd stopped to watch the passing car and then leapt away into the safety of the bush.

'It's another world here, isn't it?' Brady said in quiet admiration.

'Oh, yes….' Jo breathed in the clear, clean air. Turning her head, she curved him a smile. 'Is that what you're aiming for eventually, a place in the country?'

He made a dismissive gesture with his shoulder. 'Way too soon to have an opinion about that. I should imagine places don't come cheaply.'

'No. This farm's been in the family for years apparently. Paul and Stacey manage it for the most part and Paul's father helps when he can, but some days he's so crippled with RA he can't do much at all.'

'Rheumatoid arthritis can be a hell of a thing to live with. I struck a bit of it in Canada. Perhaps the cold climate may have had something to do with it. Is Mr Owens senior your patient?'

'Yes.'

'Has he been properly assessed?'

'Yes, of course he has.' Jo sent him a sharp look.

'There are new drugs for RA coming out all the time these days.'

'Brady, I'm well aware of that,' Jo said patiently. 'And, yes, Jack Owens has been referred to a rheumatologist. And, yes, I do see him for regular check-ups.'

'Came on a bit strong there, I guess.' A fleeting smile crossed Brady's face. 'It's just I hate to see anyone trying to lead their life surrounded with pain.'

Jo pulled him into line gently. 'Surely, as doctors, we all do.'

'Of course we do. Sorry.'

Jo stopped short of rolling her eyes, saying instead, 'You could probably park under that flame tree over there. There's plenty of shade so the car won't be too hot for Andrew when we have to leave.'

'Good thinking.' Brady adjusted his steering slightly, edging the car to a stop outside the simple timber bungalow, and switched off the engine. He removed the keys from the ignition and leaned back. Then, almost in slow motion, he turned to Jo and in a second they were looking into each other's faces.

Suddenly, there was a heaviness in the air, a sense of intimacy. Jo took a shaken breath. His mouth was close, so close, his nose and cheekbones in soft relief against the light and shadow outside the car.

Time seemed to stand still. Yet the possibility of a kiss made the air around them as thick and sultry as the air before a summer storm. And Jo knew he was thinking of it. The evidence was almost tangible in the soft glimmer of his dark eyes and the way his lips had parted to say her name on a whisper of breath.

Jo felt her heart jump every which way and deep inside her there was a sudden ache that was half pleasure and half pain. Involuntarily, she reached up, wanting to stroke the line of his lips with her fingers.

But before she could reach him, his hand captured hers and closed around it. 'Later…'

The huskiness of that one word curled around Jo like the softest silk. She shivered, and knew that he would understand exactly what her convulsive little movement meant.

His mouth compressed for a second and then he began stroking her knuckles with the ball of his thumb, sending shivers of need flooding up her arm. 'On the other hand…'

His voice was smoky and he began bending towards her slowly, so slowly...

And then the dogs interrupted, barking a welcome.

Jo gusted an off-key laugh. 'We've been sprung.'

'Seems to me, if it's not the baby, it's the dogs,' Brady said ruefully.

'Then we'd better start developing some survival skills, hadn't we? Come on.' Jo waggled a finger past his nose to the side window. 'Here come Stacey and Paul to meet us.'

'It's really good of you to come, Dr Rutherford,' Stacey said shyly as they met up at the car.

'Stacey, it's our pleasure.' Jo smiled. 'And, please, let's use first names. We're here as friends.'

'OK. Thanks.' Stacey gave a little awkward nod towards Brady. 'This is my husband, Paul,' she said. 'Paul, this is Dr...I'm sorry, I can't remember your last name.'

'NcNeal.' Brady's handshake with the young farmer was firm. 'But Brady's fine. As Jo said, we just want to help where we can.' He took a step back as the dogs began to nose inquisitively around him.

'Sorry.' Paul grimaced and gave the dogs a command that had them disappearing away towards the barn. 'They're blue heelers,' he explained, mentioning the Australian breed of cattle dog. 'Seeing we've no cows here, they're inclined to "heel" people instead. But they're very loyal and keep an eye on Lachie when Stace and I are busy with the cultivation.'

'So, what are you about to harvest at the moment?' Brady looked with something like pleasure at the luscious-looking green of the crops that were visible in paddocks that ran down the side of the hill on either side of the house.

'Beans.' Paul shifted his bush hat to the back of his head. 'We start picking next week.'

'Tough work, I imagine, bent over all day?'

'Yeah.' Paul returned Brady's wry grin. 'But we employ backpackers mostly, young students.'

Brady nodded. 'Good call.'

'We'll be ready to pick the beetroot pretty soon as well.' Paul indicated the rows and rows of distinctive dark green leaves with their purple stalks. 'We sell those to the cannery.'

'Cropping must be pretty intensive kind of work.' Brady folded his arms, screwing up his eyes and looking thoughtfully into the distance.

'If we want to keep it a family farm, we have to all pull our weight,' Paul said. 'We'd hate for one of those giant multinationals to get hold of it. It's *our* place and I hope it will be Lachie's one day.' He dipped his head, looking faintly embarrassed, as though he'd come on too strong. 'Uh, I was about to turn on the irrigation. Like a walk, Doc?'

'Yes, sure.' The two moved off companionably.

'Brady—the baby!' Jo called in disbelief after him.

He turned and smiled innocently. 'I'm sure you'll take great care of him, Jo.'

'I'm about to put the kettle on, Paul.' Stacey looked helplessly after her husband.

He turned and flicked a wave in acknowledgement. 'Won't be long, love.'

Stacey gave an inelegant little snort. 'And I'd like a dollar for every time I've heard that.'

'They're men.' Jo chuckled. 'No sense of time.' Turning, she opened the back door of the car. 'Come on, sweetheart,' she cooed, releasing the seat belt around the carry-capsule and lifting the baby out. 'This is Andrew,' she said, and there was a catch in her voice.

Stacey blinked a bit. 'Whose baby?'

'Brady's. He's a single dad.'

'Really?' Stacey's hand went to her heart. 'Does he manage OK?'

'Seems to. With the help of a carer, of course.'

'He's gorgeous,' Stacey crooned, and looked wistful. 'I'd love another baby...'

'It'll happen for you, Stacey,' Jo said quietly, and felt her own need for a child of her own widen to a river. She stifled a sigh. A man to love and a baby together. Surely it wasn't too much to ask?

'Where's Lachlan?' They were in the kitchen and Jo was cuddling AJ on her lap while his little hands were exploring the tiny soft toy she'd brought for him.

'He's watching a video.' Stacey went on preparing what looked like a feast for afternoon tea. 'It's his favourite one, *Wind in the Willows.*'

'Oh, I used to *love* that story when I was a child,' Jo sighed nostalgically. 'But the characters are quite complex, aren't they?'

'I'm sure Lachlan gets the gist of it.' Stacey's tone was slightly stiff and brittle. 'People think because his face is all funny and he can't speak properly...well, they think he's a bit slow. But he's not.'

'Of course he's not.' Jo cringed inside. She should have been more careful in her choice of words and not left her statement open to the kind of interpretation Stacey had put on them. 'No one who knows Lachie would think that.' Jo tried quickly to cover her lapse. 'And those who don't— well, you don't have to prove anything to them, do you?'

Stacey gave the semblance of a smile. 'S'pose not...'

* * *

'Well, that went pretty well, I thought.' Brady flicked Jo an enquiring look as they left the Owenses' farm. 'Lachie's a great little guy, isn't he?'

'Yes, he's special,' Jo agreed softly. 'And he was quite taken with the photos. Wasn't it precious when he grabbed his mum's arm and said, "That's me!"?'

'Mmm.' Brady's mouth tightened for a moment. It had indeed been a moving moment when the little boy had readily identified with Will's 'before' photo. Even though his acknowledgement had come out as something like, 'Nat nee'.

Jo looked thoughtful. 'This next op should see him much closer to having a regular face. It was a brilliant idea of yours to get the photos.'

'They're a great little family.' Brady eased the car through the farm gates and back onto the bitumen. 'Let's hope everything works out for them and their boy.'

It was Friday of the following week and Vicki popped her head into Jo's office. 'We've just had a call from the after-hours clinic. One of the on-call doctors can't make it this weekend—family crisis or something. They wondered if you could replace him and he'll do your shift next weekend.'

Jo took a moment to think about it. She hadn't anything planned—or not really. 'Who would I be on with?'

'Brady.'

Jo's heart gave a funny little glitch. Well, that was a turn-up. She and Brady hadn't managed to connect out of work hours since their visit to the Owenses' farm. She sent Vicki a brief smile. 'That's fine, Vic. I'll cover.'

'Thanks, Jo.' Vicki flapped a wave. 'I'll let them know.'

With Vicki gone, Jo got to her feet and stretched, her mind running back to last weekend after they'd left the farm.

It had been early evening when they'd got back to town and Brady had let her off at her house. 'Come over and have dinner with me.' His hand had reached out to snag her wrist as she'd been about to get out of the car. 'I've a couple of steaks we can barbecue.'

'Um…OK…' Jo had looked down to where his hand had curved over her wrist. 'But don't bother cooking, I'll bring a take-away. See you in an hour or so?'

'Sounds good. I'll bath AJ and feed him. He should go straight down. Time for me to have a shower and open the wine.'

The picture his words had conjured up made Jo stare at him mistily. Perhaps they'd be able to recapture the earlier mood before the dogs had so rudely interrupted them at the farm. 'I might manage it in less than an hour.'

'Excellent.' Brady crinkled a smile at her and let her hand go.

Jo hurried inside to shower and was almost dressed when her phone rang. She gave a little groan of frustration. Surely it wasn't Brady, crying off. But it wasn't. Jo listened for several minutes before ending the call, only to reactivate the dial tone and punch out Brady's number.

'McNeal.'

'Hi, it's me. About dinner…'

He chuckled. 'I'm in the mood to take a bite of anything. Just get here…'

His low, suggestively teasing comment had her thoughts whirling giddily. Jo's fingers tightened on the phone. 'This is awful, Brady, but I'm going to have to take a rain-check. One of my patients has gone into labour. She'd been helping her husband pack beans all day and thought it was just backache.'

'But obviously it's not.'

'No. And it's her first baby and she's early. They're in a bit of a panic so I have to be there.'

'Ah, well, that's the life of a country doctor, I guess.' His tone was softly wry. 'I'll open a can of beans.'

'Glad you have back-up,' she murmured through a throaty laugh. 'I guess we'll catch up some time…'

'I'm not going anywhere, Doc. Take care,' he added softly, before he hung up.

But they still hadn't caught up properly. It was beginning to feel like ships that passed in the night, Jo decided wryly.

But perhaps, if they weren't too busy at the after-hours clinic tomorrow, there'd be time to at least have a conversation that was not medically orientated.

'Bleak old day,' Brady said when they met up outside the clinic the next morning. 'Looks like rain.'

'Very unseasonable for September,' Jo agreed.

'Except it's October.'

'Is it?' Jo's eyes flashed disbelief. 'I must have lost track of time somewhere,' she added ruefully, lifting a hand to the bell at the staff entrance.

'First of the month today,' Brady confirmed, tucking his chin into the collar of his roll-necked jumper.

'Oh, lord, it's Sophie's birthday! Hi, Cheryl.' Jo smiled at the receptionist who let them in. 'I must call her before I get busy.'

'They're back from their honeymoon, then?'

'Oh, yes. They only had a week. Speaking of weddings,

I had a lovely photo from Soph in the mail this week. It was of her and Ben, walking hand in hand through the botanic gardens after the ceremony. It was specially developed in a sepia tone, looked really old-fashioned and gorgeous.' Jo rolled her eyes and laughed. 'So *Sophie*.'

'There's probably one waiting for me at my parents' place.' Brady followed her inside. 'I haven't actually caught up with Ben to give him my address here. The wedding seems ages ago, doesn't it?'

Jo nodded. And such a lot had happened since that day. The day she and Brady had met for the first time.

The receptionist, Cheryl Chalmers, showed them to their allotted rooms, which were situated side by side. 'I think you'll find everything you need.' She smiled at Jo. 'Thank you for filling in at short notice, Dr Rutherford.'

'It's fine,' Jo dismissed.

Cheryl turned to Brady and said pleasantly, 'I understand it's your first time here, Dr McNeal.'

'Yes.' Brady's mouth compressed briefly. 'What kind of cases do we handle?'

'The service provides treatment for minor emergencies only,' Cheryl said. 'The kind of thing folk would normally pop along to see their regular GP about.'

Jo's mouth tucked in on a grin. 'Expect anything from headache to diarrhea, with a few bumps and sprains thrown in for good measure.'

Brady laughed and then drawled, 'So, just a regular day at the office.'

Cheryl came in quickly, 'We try to schedule appointments so the doctors are able to get away by four-thirty where possible. Sometimes it works, sometimes it doesn't. But we do try. Now, I'll leave you to get settled. If you need anything, Dr McNeal, just hit one and zero on your phone pad. That'll connect you with Reception.'

Brady nodded. 'Thanks, Cheryl. I'll remember that.'

As they parted to go to their separate rooms, Jo turned and asked, 'Thea OK about the weekend?'

Brady stopped with his shoulder against the door. 'Looking forward to it, she said.' His mouth twitched. 'She and AJ are making gingerbread men, I believe.'

Jo's chuckle was warm. 'Advanced son you have there, Doctor.' Fluttering a wave, she disappeared into her consulting room.

Brady began making himself at home in the borrowed office. It was well equipped but impersonal, as he'd expected.

Putting a few of his own bits and pieces on the desk, he strolled across to the window and looked out. The rain had begun to fall, sheeting down quite heavily. Coming in off the mountains, he assumed.

He wondered if the district was prone to flooding. If so, they could be in for some extra work over the weekend. In his experience, people notoriously seemed to throw caution to the winds during unfamiliar weather patterns and took crazy chances with vehicles and their own personal safety.

Jo rearranged things on the desk to her liking, feeling a huge lift in her spirits. It was nice to feel at ease with Brady again. She just hoped it would last.

Sorting out a prescription pad in readiness, she located anything else she might possibly need and decided while she had a moment she'd call Sophie and wish her a happy birthday.

CHAPTER EIGHT

SOMETHING didn't add up here. Jo frowned slightly as she unwound the blood-pressure cuff from her patient's arm. Georgia Whiting was her last patient for the day and experience was telling Jo the sixteen-year-old was concerned about something more than the bad headache she'd supposedly come about.

'How often are you getting the headaches?' Jo asked.

'Pretty often.'

Then why on earth hadn't this young person sought help from her own GP before now? Jo wondered. She knew she could just give her patient something for her headache and let her go, but something held Jo back and instead she asked, 'Do you get pain connected with your periods?'

Georgia hesitated. 'Sometimes...'

'Are they regular?'

'They used to be. I haven't had one for a couple of months.'

'There's no chance you could be pregnant?' Jo asked carefully.

'No way.' Georgia gave a little huff of derision. 'I don't even have a boyfriend.'

Jo's mouth made a moue of conjecture. 'Just pop up on the scales for me, please, Georgia.'

The teenager eyed Jo warily and seemed to shrink back within herself. 'I told you, I have a headache.'

'You also appear quite a bit underweight for your height,' Jo responded calmly. 'If we're to find out the cause of your headaches, we need to have an overall picture of your general health. That makes sense, doesn't it?'

Georgia jerked a shoulder dismissively. 'Why can't you just give me a script for something I can get at the chemist?'

'Because until we know the cause of your headaches, that option could be quite dangerous. Now, for starters, let's see what you weigh.'

Reluctantly, Georgia got to her feet and stepped gingerly onto the scales, staying only long enough for Jo to note that her weight was forty-two kilograms.

Jo did some calculations quickly. She judged Georgia's height to be around five feet six inches. At that rate, her body mass index was quite a bit below what it should have been.

Suddenly she sensed a much bigger problem.

But softly, softly. First she would have to get her patient's trust and then and only then could she begin to get at the real cause of Georgia's problems.

Thoughtfully, Jo put down the pen she'd been tapping end to end on the top of the desk. 'Georgia, I think we need to look into the state of your health far more closely. Do you have a GP you normally go to?'

The girl shook her head. 'We haven't been here very long.'

'I see. Would you be prepared to come and see me at my regular surgery at Mt Pryde Medical Centre?'

The girl hesitated. 'Would I have to tell my mum?'

'Not if you don't want to. But it would be good if you felt you could. When we're going through a rough patch, our mums are usually pretty good at helping to sort things out.'

Georgia lowered her fair head, interlinking her fingers in a tight little knot. 'I'm a mess,' she murmured hoarsely.

It had taken quite a deal of courage for her to have admitted that, and even more to have fronted here at the after-hours clinic today. 'Nothing is so bad it can't be fixed,' Jo said kindly. 'At least, we'll give it a darned good try. But we can't fix anything here today. This surgery is for mild emergencies only. You'll need to see me on a regular basis if we're going to get you the kind of help you need. Now…' Jo beamed a disarming smile. 'Can I expect to see you on Monday?'

Georgia swallowed unevenly. 'I'll…come after school. Will that be OK?'

'Perfectly. I'll make sure our receptionist fits you in.'

'I came here last weekend,' Georgia said, the words tumbling out. 'But there were only male doctors working and I didn't want to speak to a man.'

'Well, I'm glad you came back today.' Jo got to her feet. 'Now, I'm going to give you some medication for your headache and I want you wait here for a while so I can monitor you. Is that OK?'

The youngster lowered her head and wrapped her arms tightly around her midriff. 'Do you think I'm a nut case?'

'No.' Jo touched her on the shoulder as she went across to the drugs cabinet. 'I think you're a very brave lady.'

The rain was still falling when Brady left the clinic. He'd hung about waiting for Jo but obviously she was still with a patient.

He was disappointed. He'd intended to ask her for a quiet drink after they'd finished surgery. Just the two of them without the baby in tow. Not that he wasn't crazy about his son, but sometimes lately he'd felt the need to escape the onerous routine of parenthood.

He gunned the motor, easing his car towards the exit and thought wryly that he understood now why the parents of young children craved some 'me' time. Well, it wasn't going to happen tonight. The weather was filthy. He couldn't expect Jo to turn out again after a long day of listening to other people's problems and start listening to his.

But on the other hand they didn't necessarily have to discuss anyone's problems, did they…?

Standing at the counter at Reception, Jo watched through the glass doors as Georgia climbed into the cab Jo had insisted on calling and paying for.

She just hoped Georgia would keep her appointment on Monday. Even from her very cursory consultation with the youngster, Jo knew there were multi-layered problems to sort out. Stifling a sigh, she signed the doctors' attendance book and handed it back to Cheryl. 'Dr McNeal get away on time?'

'Pretty much.'

Jo was glad. He'd be anxious to get home to relieve Thea and spend time with his little boy.

'Sorry to have kept *you* late, though.' Cheryl was hovering a bit restlessly, obviously anxious to lock up and be on her own way home.

'Not a problem, Cheryl.' Jo hitched her medical bag off the counter. 'I don't have any plans for this evening.' More's the pity, she lamented silently.

Cheryl began snapping off lights. 'Not the kind of night to be going out, anyway.' She tilted a dry smile. 'I'm hoping my husband will have a nice fire going when I get home. And even begun a meal if I'm halfway lucky.'

They left the building together, calling goodbye, as they each ran for their separate vehicles.

Jo drove slowly home, taking her usual route along the main street. But tonight it seemed eerily deserted, with only her car's headlights burnishing the darkened windows of the shops.

Lucky Cheryl, she thought, her mouth drooping dispiritedly. Going home to a warm house, a meal on the way… Jo's thoughts went to Sophie, blissfully happy in her marriage to Ben. Perhaps that's what I need, she decided, a man about the house.

The idea buzzed around in her head and she bit off a huff of impatience at her crazy thinking.

As she drove into her carport, she was still thinking about it. But now her thoughts had gone way ahead and she realised she wanted more than a just a man about the house.

Much more.

There was one message on her answering-machine. Jo flicked the button to listen, hoping she wouldn't have to turn out in the rain again.

'Hi—it's me.'

She recognised Brady's voice and automatically bent closer, sinking down on the little chair beside her phone table. She was still in her raincoat, several tendrils of fair hair plastered across her cheekbones from her dash to the car in the rain.

'Uh, I know it's a foul night but I wondered if you'd like to eat with me. Thea's left some kind of casserole. It smells fantastic. Anyway, if you've nothing planned… Uh, I've got a fire going. Call me if you can make it.'

Jo felt her spirits lift to the ceiling. It was almost as if Brady had tapped into her own thoughts. Did he want to be with her as much as she wanted to be with him? Her eyes closed for a second, sensation focusing, then diffusing, until a slow, languid warmth enveloped her and desire grew and expanded like a living thing.

Oh, lord. Taking a shaken breath, she reached out and picked up the phone. 'Hi, it's me,' she said when he answered. 'I've just got in.'

'Ah. Long consult?'

'Complicated,' she replied. 'Your offer of dinner still on?'

'You betcha. Coming over?'

The hopeful lilt in his voice almost undid her. 'Give me a few minutes to have a shower and I'll be there.'

'Good. I'll open the wine—red, I think. Drive carefully,' he added throatily.

Jo replaced the phone slowly. Driving rain or not, wise or not, she had to go to him.

Freshly showered, a towel wrapped loosely around her, she reached out and palmed the mist away from the bathroom mirror. Her face, the face she looked at every day, seemed different, with eyes that were too large, an unfamiliar wanton expression hazing their greenness.

Her fingers clenched over the tucked-in towel between the hollow of her breasts. Where on earth do you think you're going with this? she demanded silently of her reflection, suddenly afraid of how badly she wanted Brady.

Swinging decisively away from the mirror, she stepped into the bedroom, flicking through the clothes in her wardrobe. Obviously, the most sensible idea would have been to pull on a pair of jeans and snuggle into a sweater, but her odd mood wouldn't allow that.

Instead, she chose a longish, silk jersey dress in a dusky red, its slim-line cut skimming all the right places.

Later, looking at herself in the full-length mirror, Jo

took a ragged breath. She felt almost giddy with excitement. 'OK, calm down,' she told herself severely, as she collected her umbrella and keys and made her way out through the laundry to the carport.

Brady had obviously been watching out for her. As Jo pulled into his driveway, she saw him silhouetted against the porch light. Her heart began a drumbeat in her chest. She switched off the ignition and for a second she closed her eyes and gave in to everything she was feeling.

But the indulgence she'd allowed herself was wafted away by Brady's swift arrival beside her car. He tapped on her driver's window, indicating the outsized umbrella he was wielding over his head and waving away the use of her own small one. 'I've got you covered,' he insisted, as she swung out of the car. Sliding his arm around her, he held her close to his side and walked her quickly across the lawn to the shelter of the front verandah.

'Wow!' In the light from the porch lantern, Brady's eyes took their fill of his dinner guest and then he frowned slightly. 'You're not wet, are you?'

'Just caught a few raindrops. Nothing to worry about.'

'Good. You look lovely, by the way.'

Jo gave a stilted laugh. 'Just felt like dressing up a bit.'

And that was a huge understatement. Brady all but groaned, wild need, a man's need, racing through him like an express train. He took a moment to compose his thoughts, anchoring the umbrella to dry at the end of the verandah. Then he said briskly, 'Please, come in, Jo. Everything's set out in the kitchen.' He led the way through. 'I, uh, thought we'd eat out there. It's kind of cosy.'

'Fine. Something smells good,' she said with a strained smile.

'Told you.' He flashed her a crooked grin. 'Glass of wine?'

'Mmm. Anything I can do to help?'

'There's very little to do,' he said, pouring the wine and handing her a glass. 'It's just nice to have company.'

He was right about that. Jo nibbled the edge of her lower lip. Odd, though, her evenings had never felt lonely before. Now, suddenly being alone equated with being lonely.

Just since this man and his baby had stepped into her life. 'AJ asleep?'

He nodded. 'Went out like a light. I think the rain on the tin roof lulled him. We shouldn't be interrupted.'

Like last time. When they'd kissed.

Lord, it felt good to have her here. Brady picked up his glass and looked at her over its rim. Better than good.

He took a mouthful of the full-bodied wine, desire, blade-sharp, stabbing him out of nowhere, bringing with it a replay of the last time she'd been here, when their hands and mouths had said so much more than words ever could...

He put his wine down with a careless little thump. 'Let's eat, shall we? You must be starved.' Grabbing a teatowel, he turned and opened the warming oven.

'I think you're supposed to use this.' Jo stepped up beside him, waggling the oven mitt.

He looked baffled.

'So you can hold hot things, like casserole dishes, and not burn your hands,' she explained blandly.

'Ah, I wondered what they were for.'

'What, your hands?'

'Joker.' He snorted a husky laugh. 'Get some plates down, huh? They're the big round things on the shelf over there.'

Jo wrinkled her nose at him. 'The food smells heaven-ly,' she said, watching as he set the dish on the tabletop and removed the lid.

'I think we've already established that.' Hell, he was acting like a lunatic. He drew in a steadying breath. 'Would you serve? I seem to be all thumbs—but not all *burned* thumbs, thanks to you.'

'You'll know next time.' She gave a fluttery laugh. He was nervous about this evening, too, she thought in amaze-ment, and immediately felt better. It meant he cared.

They made inconsequential conversation during the meal. Brady asked about her day and she returned the com-pliment. Finally, Jo said after an awkward little lull, 'The meal was delicious, Brady. Thank you.'

'Thank you for sharing it with me.' He swiped the ser-viette around his mouth, his movement forced and a bit jerky. 'But we should both be thanking Thea.'

'Did she get the gingerbread men made?' Jo asked.

'Mmm. Apparently, they're for the church fête next weekend. But she left us a couple to taste-test.'

'Can't wait.' Jo laughed and their gazes met and clung. It was such a silly conversation. In fact, the whole evening had held an air of silliness, of unreality. But at least now, after the food, they'd both begun to relax.

But as if to negate all that, she caught Brady's look, so warm, so heavy, and knew the wildness of her feelings would be back again, only this time exacerbated by this subtle air of cosiness he'd referred to. She got to her feet quickly. 'I'll make some coffee, shall I?'

When the coffee was made, they took it through to the lounge room. 'Did you bring the gingerbread biscuits?' Jo asked, setting the tray on the long table in front of the fire.

'You mean the gingerbread *men*.' Brady pulled a face. 'What parts are we supposed to eat first, do you suppose?'

'Idiot,' Jo said with a chuckle, settling herself beside him on the divan and pouring the coffee. 'Actually, I think it's permissible to dunk them in your coffee,' she said with a chuckle.

'Like this?' He picked up one of the shapes, dipped it in his coffee and held it out to her. 'Open wide, like a good little bird,' he said. She opened her mouth on a laugh and he put the gingerbread in, his fingers brushing her lips as he did so.

Gaze narrowed, Brady watched as a slow drugging heat spilled into her eyes and her breath seemed suddenly shallow. All that was male in him convulsed, desire, fierce and unrelenting, gripping his insides like tentacles. He took a breath so deep it hurt, his jaw tightening as he turned away, tossing the gingerbread back onto its glass plate. 'Let's stop this silly game,' he said gruffly, and drew her into his arms.

She came without stopping to consider what her capitulation might mean, her body turning so that she lay across his lap, her head nestling in the crook of his shoulder, looking up at him.

Brady took a swift, indrawn breath. The V of her neckline was gaping slightly, revealing the shadow between her breasts. 'Jo…' His mouth lowered to her throat, his lips on the tiny pulse point that beat frantically in the hollow above her collar-bone. 'I've wanted to be with you like this so much.'

'Me, too…' she murmured, and reached up to stroke along his jaw and up into his hairline at the base of his neck.

He drew back to look at her, running the tip of his finger across the soft curve of her bottom lip. 'I'd been thinking about asking you for dinner all day. I shouldn't have hesitated.'

'I thought about you on the way home.'

'Did you?'

'Mmm.' Her throat was so dry she could hardly make a sound. 'Cheryl talked about going home to her husband and a fire and a hot meal. And I thought about going home alone to no one.'

'Ah, Jo.' He looked at her for a long moment, unable to tear his eyes away from the soft mistiness in hers. 'You're here now. That's all that matters...' His voice caught as he swallowed.

Jo's heart beat so heavily, she could feel it thundering in her chest.   'So, now that we *are* here...together...?'

He nodded, seeming to understand what she was asking. Sliding his arms around her, he lifted her as though she weighed no more than an armful of roses and brought her up with him to her feet.

Very slowly, they pulled back, waiting there a moment, staring into each other's eyes. 'Stay with me tonight,' he said, his voice deep and not quite even.

Jo felt desire rock through her, her nod of assent almost imperceptible, and together they moved across to his bedroom and he closed the door.

'What about Andrew?' Jo forced her thoughts back to something like reality. 'Will we hear him if he cries?'

'I've got one of those monitor things next to my bed.'

'Oh, OK.' Jo looked around her, her eyes taking in the softly lit space, one bedside lamp giving out a soft glow of light across the pillow.

Brady made a deep sound in his throat that could have been a sigh. Then he reached for her, cupping her shoulders and drawing her in against him, lowering his mouth to taste her lips.

That was all it took. Like a spark on straw, the fire caught hold and within milliseconds it was raging.

With a ragged groan he took her mouth, ravishing it, as though to quench the thirst of a lifetime. And she responded with a need of her own, pressing herself against him.

Brady whispered harshly against her mouth, 'I meant to take it easy—be gentle with you.'

Jo moaned. There was nothing gentle about this. But she didn't want gentle. She welcomed the almost savage thoroughness with which he took her mouth over and over.

But she craved an even closer contact, leaning into him so that every tiny space between them was taken up and filled. When Brady finally lifted his head, she could hardly stand, and stayed there with her arms wrapped around him for support.

'Jo…sweetheart…' Brady whispered against her hair. 'Please, be sure about this…'

She arched back with a little cry. 'Of course I'm sure.' Her hands threaded through his hair, and she trapped his face, holding him. 'Are you unsure?'

He turned his head and gently nipped the soft flesh below her thumb, softly amused when she gasped an indrawn breath. 'Does it look like it?'

Together they fumbled over buttons and zippers, Brady swearing over shoelaces and socks. And then he stepped back, raking his eyes over her. 'You're beautiful…'

Her smile was a little unsteady and she reached up to run the tips of her fingers down over his chest and lower…

'Wait!' He jumped away and suddenly the tension was unbearable. He began looking blindly around. 'I…have to protect you.'

Jo wrapped her arms around her body. Leave it, she

wanted to plead with him, almost over the edge, yearning to feel him inside her, feel his seed spilling into her.

'Just make love with me,' she begged in a ragged whisper. Oh, God… He was unable to resist her any longer.

Instinctively, he knew just what would please her, excite her. And when she cried out, the first ripples of her release beginning, he looked down at her and knew he couldn't hold back any longer.

And in an instant he was freefalling over the precipice, fuelled by the wondrous feel of her, the fusion of their two bodies, their two spirits. Into somewhere like heaven just made for the two of them.

Jo woke about six when a persistent sunbeam found its way through a chink in the blind and stole across the pillow to her face.

Raising herself on one elbow, she looked at the man beside her. Brady was still fast asleep. He was sprawled on his back, one arm thrown at right angles beside his head, totally relaxed.

She smiled. They'd made love again during the night and it had been absolutely special. But gentler the second time around. Gentler and, perhaps in ways too subtle to analyse, more meaningful.

Seconds later, a little snuffling sound on the baby monitor had Jo sliding carefully out of bed.

Almost an hour later, Brady found her on the back deck with his son.

'Good morning, sleepyhead.' Jo wanted to spring up from her chair and straight into his arms, but something in his expression held her back. 'You OK?'

A fleeting frown crossed his face. 'You should have woken me.'

'Why?' She looked up at him, her eyes puzzled. 'Andrew and I have managed just fine. I've changed him and fed him and now, as you see, he seems perfectly content.'

Brady felt ruffled inside, out of kilter. But he couldn't find fault with Jo's care of his son. AJ looked amazingly happy, moving gently in the padded baby swing near her feet, his little legs kicking happily and his eyes bright and interested as he gazed around his untroubled world.

So why the hell did *he* feel so put out?

'I thought you'd welcome a sleep-in.'

'That wasn't necessary,' he said shortly.

Jo blinked uncertainly. Why was he being so defensive about things? She'd thought she was helping but obviously, according to Brady, she wasn't. She couldn't understand the reason for his attitude. And it seemed he wasn't about to enlighten her. 'I, uh, borrowed one of your shirts— I hope that was all right?' she said pithily.

'Of course it was,' he dismissed. 'And, Jo, thanks.' His mouth worked for a moment. 'But, honestly, you shouldn't have let me sleep.'

A beat of silence.

Jo spread her hands in a helpless gesture as she got to her feet. This conversation was getting them nowhere. She felt sick to her stomach. Brady wasn't acting like a lover. In fact, he was backtracking so fast he'd fall over if he wasn't careful.

Quite obviously their love-making hadn't stopped his world the way it had stopped hers... She swallowed the lump in her throat. 'Water's just boiled if you want tea. I'll change and be on my way.' She pushed her canvas chair in. 'It's...turned out to be a lovely morning.'

'Yes.' Well, it had been until he'd stuck his great foot in

his mouth. 'Jo.' He spun to face her, an almost feverish sheen in his eyes. 'Look, you don't have to leave. Stay and have breakfast.'

Jo's bitter laugh fell around them like fragments of glass. 'I don't think so, Brady. I don't believe in putting my head on the chopping block twice. And in case you've forgotten, it's a nine-thirty start at the clinic today.' Without a backward glance she walked inside and shortly after that he heard her car start and reverse out of his driveway.

Why had he let her go like that? Because he was some kind of idiot. Brady's hands gripped his tea-mug like a lifeline and he looked sightlessly out across the back garden.

Jo Rutherford was the truest thing that had come into his life for the longest time. And their love-making had been magical. But now, thanks to his total lack of sensitivity, his inability to put things in their right perspective, she was probably feeling used. And he couldn't blame her. He made a muted sound of disgust. 'Pathetic' would be too fine a word to use about his behaviour.

Damn it! he raged silently. Why on earth hadn't he been prepared to follow through on what he'd started? And where would it all end...?

CHAPTER NINE

Jo CLAMPED down on her bottom lip, just keeping the tears at bay until she got home.

She'd given her heart to Brady on a platter. And her body. And this morning he'd chucked them right back at her. Yet, deep within her, she knew what they'd shared had been amazing, incredible, special and all the superlatives under the sun.

But now whatever they'd shared was shattered irrevocably. He didn't want her in his real life. Like a fool, she'd imagined that after what they'd been to each other last night, she'd automatically be invited in. But apparently she'd got it all wrong and this morning she'd blundered over some invisible line, not knowing it had been there.

Now it was as clear as the nose on her face. Brady regretted everything. Perhaps he'd even gone so far as to fantasise he'd been making love with *Tanya* last night. The thought made her feel sick. But there was no getting away from the fact. His hostile reaction this morning could mean only one thing—he was still in love with the mother of his son.

Stiffly, her body shocked and exhausted by emotion, she

got out of the car and let herself into the house. The house she'd left last night in such anticipation, her need to be with him flowing over.

In the shower, she let the water pour over her head, squeezing her eyes shut against the tears, but they wouldn't stop coming, mingling with the shower spray, while she sobbed as though her heart would break.

Jo had her emotions well under control by the time she arrived at the clinic. She was early, resolving to do what she had to do—to survive the day. Even if it meant staying in her room until the last patient had gone.

Brady McNeal was history. He could carry his own damned baggage from now on. But she felt almost grief-stricken that her decision meant also that she would have to sever all contact with his baby son.

She gave an automatic smile when Cheryl let her in, agreed it had turned out nice after the rain and yes, she'd love a cup of tea, thank you.

Brady looked warily at Thea when she asked him if he was feeling all right. 'Of course I am,' he said shortly. 'Do I look sick?'

'Just a bit distracted.' Undeterred, Thea went on stirring her coffee. 'Were you up with Andrew during the night?'

'No, he was fine.' Brady was searching vainly for his car keys. But Thea was right. He *was* distracted. He ticked off everything he'd done since Jo had walked out earlier. Like throwing his sheets into the washing machine and remaking the bed. And going into the lounge room and getting rid of the coffee they hadn't drunk, and discarding the gingerbread. The damned gingerbread. The hollow feeling in his stomach intensified. That's when everything had jackknifed out of control.

He found his keys at last. 'I'll be off now, Thea,' he said shortly. 'I shouldn't be late.'

'Don't rush home on my account.' Thea sent him an old-fashioned look. 'Why don't you have a bit of down-time? Take Jo for a drink or something?'

And her accepting was about as likely as winning Lotto without taking a ticket. Brady's heart wrenched. He'd be very surprised if Jo Rutherford ever wanted to speak to him again. But somehow he'd have to try to explain his actions—make her listen. Somehow.

By mid-afternoon, Jo knew her plan for avoiding Brady was succeeding. But she fully admitted the four walls of her consulting room had begun to feel like a prison and when her next appointment cancelled, she took a chance and ducked out to the staffroom for a change of scene.

But her heart fell in a heap when she pushed open the door and found Brady there. He was standing at the window, staring out, the thumb of one hand hooked in the side pocket of his jeans, the other nursing a mug of coffee against his chest. There was a crippling breath of silence as they confronted one another. Then Brady took the initiative.

'Taking a break?'

'Obviously,' she replied thinly. 'Any coffee left?'

'On its last legs. I'd make instant if I were you.'

She swallowed a bitter laugh. 'Now, there's something to contemplate. *If you were me.*'

His mouth moved in a travesty of a smile. 'I'd think I'd want to beat the hell out of me.'

Jo's heart began revving sickeningly fast. 'Lucky for

you I'm not a violent person, then. On second thoughts, I don't think I'll worry about the coffee.'

'Jo…' He paused awkwardly. 'I need to talk to you.'

She sent him a flinty look. 'I'm not available to listen, Brady. Go talk to a counsellor.' *I don't need you messing up my life, the way you've messed up your own*, she felt like hurling at him but somehow she just couldn't. She ducked her head, avoiding the hurt in his eyes. He looked as shocked as if she'd slapped him.

Ignoring the shaking in her knees, she reached blindly for the door, wrenching it open and almost falling over Cheryl in the process. 'Oh—sorry!' Jo's hand went to the other's shoulder. 'I wasn't looking.'

Cheryl waved away her concern. 'We've had an emergency call from the ambulance base.' She darted a worried look between the two doctors.

Brady's head swung round. 'Problem, Cheryl?' Ditching his coffee down the sink, he looked questioningly at the receptionist.

'Sounds like it.' Cheryl came into the room. 'According to the information the base has, there's a party of bush walkers who've come to grief at Flinder's Gorge.'

'How, exactly, come to grief?' Brady snapped with barely concealed impatience.

'A landslide of some kind.'

'Oh, lord…' Jo felt the nerves in her stomach clench.

Brady shot her a sharp look. 'How far is this Flinder's Gorge?'

'It's a tourist spot—about twenty Ks,' Jo informed him, and looked at Cheryl for further clarification of the situation. 'Do we know how many and what kinds of injuries?'

Cheryl shook her head. 'The base said it was a mobile

phone and the connection was a bit iffy. They'll ring back as soon as they have more information. But in the meantime they've put in a request for a couple of doctors to get out there.'

Jo's brow pleated in a quick frown. 'That's usually a job for the emergency department at the hospital.'

'Apparently they're fully occupied with a road trauma. They can't spare anyone.'

'So, looks like we're it, then, Dr Rutherford.' Brady's mouth twisted with faint mockery.

She'd rather stick needles in her eyes than have to spend the rest of the day with him, Jo decided grimly. But they were doctors and they had no choice than to answer the call.

'Oh—there's the phone. It might be the base again.' Cheryl bolted, with Jo and Brady hurrying after her.

'If it is, I'll speak to them,' Brady said with quiet authority. 'The sooner we know what we're dealing with, the better.'

The call was indeed from the ambulance base and Cheryl handed the receiver across to Brady.

Arms folded tightly across her torso, Jo listened while he fired questions into the mouthpiece. Gradually it dawned on her that with every question he was getting a clearer picture of the emergency they were facing. He was good, she had to admit. And obviously quite unfazed by what he was hearing.

Suddenly, most of her personal animosity faded. And she felt relief beyond words that Brady had taken over. Somehow, between them, they'd handle this rescue like the trained medical officers they were.

'OK, it's a bit clearer now.' Brady slammed the receiver down. 'It's actually a church youth group involved. Two leaders, six youngsters.'

Jo's hand went to her throat. 'Kids?'

'Young teenagers. They're from Brisbane. Drove up yesterday and made it safely to the huts provided. But because of the weather they were pretty much confined. So this morning, when it looked like such a good day for hiking, they set out along one of the trails down through the gorge.'

'And a wall collapsed?'

'Something like that. Anyway, we'd better get moving. We'll take my car,' he added, his tone brooking no argument.

Jo didn't argue, agreeing silently it was a good decision. His heavier vehicle would handle the current uncertain road conditions more safely than her own smaller sedan.

'So, what's the drill?' Brady shot the question at Jo, dark brows lifted in query. 'Do we collect a trauma kit from the hospital?'

'That's the usual procedure.'

'Then you'd best be off,' Cheryl said briskly. 'I'll close the surgery and leave a notice on the door. There's been only a trickle of patients through since lunchtime anyway. And there's no one waiting at the moment.'

'So let's get out while we can.' Brady ran a hand through his hair, as if collating his thoughts. 'I guess I'd better give Thea a call. We could be a while.'

They arrived in the car park almost simultaneously. When Jo would have hurried on to her own car, Brady stopped her with the slightest touch on her arm. 'Would you like to shoot home first and change? I can deal with the stuff at the hospital, then swing by your place and pick you up.'

Jo looked down at her soft leather sandals and made a face. 'They'll provide us with overalls at the hospital but I could do with some more appropriate footwear, I guess.'

'OK.' Brady opened his boot and slung his medical case in. 'See you in a bit, then.'

'Uh…about this rescue…' Jo faltered, her eyes clouding with faint uncertainty. 'How are we going to get down to assess the injuries?'

Brady's dark brows beetled together. 'From what the base said, the state emergency service people are already on their way. I expect they'll have the right gear for us.'

Jo licked her lips. She knew exactly what that would entail. Ropes. A slow crawl of nerves began in her stomach. 'Can you abseil?'

He lifted a shoulder dismissively. 'Done heaps. You?'

'I'm fit,' she prevaricated. 'I'll cope.'

Brady's dark gaze tracked the sudden tautness in her body language. 'Jo, if you're not up for this, don't be a martyr. I can try Tom's mobile—see if he's available.'

Jo flared. Was he inferring that because she was female, she had to be protected in some way? 'I can pull my weight.'

'If you say so.' Brady held up his hands in mock surrender. 'Just don't try punching above it, that's all. Otherwise, on a jaunt like this, we could be placing lives in jeopardy.'

It was a sobering thought. And Jo carried it with her all the way home.

Was she being foolhardy? she agonised. If it had been a water retrieval, she wouldn't have had to think twice about her capability. She'd lived on the coast for much of her growing-up years. She was a strong swimmer. She had senior lifesaving credentials. And just recently, on her holiday, she'd helped out in a medical emergency and successfully treated a diver who had suffered the bends.

And a fat lot of good that knowledge is going to do you

now, she thought with hollow humour, pulling swiftly into her carport.

In her bedroom, she stripped, replacing the clothes she'd worn to the surgery with jeans and a fleecy top. Stopping for a second, she blew out a calming breath and began looking for a pair of walking shoes, recalling from somewhere that it was better to have footwear with a flexible sole so you could *feel* the dips and crevices beneath you as you descended.

That scenario invited a new swarm of butterflies to invade her tummy.

'*I can do this,*' she recited over and over like a mantra as she hurried outside to wait for Brady.

Sam Whittaker from the SES rescue squad was waiting for them at the top of the escarpment. Introductions were made swiftly, with Sam adding, 'Two of my team have already scaled down to the walking party. They've taken space blankets and collapsible stretches with them.'

'Do we have any more details of injuries?' Brady handed Jo a pair of the orange-coloured overalls the hospital had supplied and began shrugging into his own.

'It's an all-female group of teenagers,' Sam relayed precisely. 'One leader suspected broken leg. But until you can get down there and assess her, we can't really be sure of anything. Our base has alerted the CareFlight chopper. Should be here within the hour.'

Jo chimed in, 'If the others in the group are just walking wounded, how do we get them out?'

'We've an ambulance lined up to wait at the end of the gorge and our own troop carrier is on standby,' Sam said. 'So far, according to my lads, the main concern is for the youngster with the fracture.'

'Right. We'd better move it, then.' Brady swung a questioning look to Steve. 'You ready to fit us out, mate?'

Brady climbed into his harness as though he'd done it countless times. Jo was more circumspect, looking to Steve for guidance. 'It's a sit-in harness, Doc,' he said kindly. 'And I've used the figure-of-eight knot. Is that OK for you?'

'Fine.' She swallowed jerkily, telling herself to stay calm and trying to summon all the techniques she had ever learned. Which had been gathered precisely from one weekend of lessons years ago, when she, Sophie and Fliss had practised abseiling down an artificial wall for the fun of doing something different. She wished now she'd taken much more notice of what they'd been told.

Settling the rope between her jeans-clad legs and under her right thigh, she became sickeningly aware her heart was thumping as if it would break loose from her chest. 'Thanks,' she murmured hoarsely, accepting one of the lightweight safety helmets from Sam's outstretched hand and settling it over her head.

'So, Sam,' Brady checked the trauma kit's bulk where he'd anchored it just below his backside, 'which is the best way down?'

Sam pointed, and together they peered all the way down into the gorge, where the sun had barely seeped through. Jo suppressed a shiver, feeling only an ominous stillness.

'My guys judged this side the safest.' Palm up, Sam gestured with his hand. 'Not much damage. The fall's obviously happened over there and shaken all the way along.' He pointed to the ugly gaps in the other side of the cliff where the earth and rocks looked as though they'd been scooped away by some giant mechanical hand. 'And once you're down, you'll have roughly a twenty-minute walk to the accident scene. Craig and Jonno will have left markers for you to follow. Just be extra-careful on the descent. In this type of country, conditions can change in seconds.'

Beside him, Brady felt Jo stiffen. Instinctively, he turned to her and said quietly, 'Trust me, it looks more daunting than it actually is.' He signalled to Sam that they were ready and then his gaze narrowed on Jo. 'We'll go over together. Stay close to me. You'll be fine.'

Despite Brady's reassurance, Jo soon realised that even for the experienced the going was rough and difficult and fraught with the unexpected.

'Watch out for stuff like this. There's no foothold,' Brady warned, testing his boot against a huge grass root. Disturbed from its shallow base, the clump gave way easily, revealing a sparse, stringy root system.

Jo stilled, her mind on full alert, feeling perspiration lodge uncomfortably in the small of her back. 'I thought you said it was easy.'

'Relatively speaking, it is. And you're doing great,' he said gruffly.

Like heck she was, Jo thought grimly. Her body felt locked with tension and there was a crick in her neck that was giving her hell. But she couldn't tell Brady that. She'd already sensed he possessed the discipline of a skilled climber, and physically, powerfully built and all, he was as sure-footed as a mountain goat.

With painstaking slowness they continued to push down-wards. Just how far did they still have to go? Jo agonised, wanting the nightmare over. Daring a glance down, she reeled back, seeing only gaping space and the shape of a long gully filled with the crazed debris of the landslide.

'Oh, help.' Black nausea grabbed her and she pressed

into the cliff-face while her insides crumpled into thick mush like badly cooked porridge.

Brady swore under his breath, closing up quickly beside her. She looked the colour of parchment. 'Take some deep breaths,' he ordered. 'That's it. In and out. More yet. Keep going. You shouldn't have looked down if it's a problem. First thing you learn as a climber.'

Well, she knew that now. Her shoulders lifted in a final steadying breath. 'You've done quite a bit, haven't you?'

'With the mountain rescue in Canada. I was a trained member of the squad.'

'Oh, boy!' She gave a strangled laugh. 'You must think I'm an awful wimp…'

'We're all wimps about something.' Brady let his eyes track over her professionally. She'd regained colour but she'd had him worried there for a minute. 'I'm a wimp about frogs,' he confessed with a lopsided grin.

'But frogs are gorgeous!' Jo felt her equilibrium returning in leaps and bounds and she knew he'd started this silly conversation with just such an outcome in mind.

'There you are, then.'

She blinked uncertainly. 'I'm all right now, Brady. Thanks.'

His mouth made a twisted moue and his gaze flicked up and down. 'Just remember you're a fine doctor, Josephine Rutherford—even if you're a wimp about heights.'

She sent him a saccharine-sweet smile in return. 'And you remember you're a fine doctor as well, Brady McNeal—even if you're a wimp about frogs.'

'So we're even.' His eyes glinted briefly. 'Now, are you ready to go on?'

'Quite ready.'

'Good. Then let's knock over the rest of this descent and go save some lives.'

Jo thought her glitch would have wasted precious time but, in fact, it hadn't and they'd paused for only a minute or two. Now they'd begun again, her whole mood seemed lighter, more steady. And somehow, quite oddly and remarkably, she felt back in tune with Brady.

'The damage doesn't seem so bad this end.' They'd been making their way through the gorge for nearly twenty minutes and Jo's hopes had been rising steadily that maybe the others in the group of bush walkers had escaped with minor injuries.

'Maybe the girl with the fracture was just unlucky. Caught a hit from a rock fall or something similar. We'll know in a minute.' Brady touched her arm. 'There's our lookout.'

Brady acknowledged the two men from the SES team as they came forward to meet them. 'I'm Brady McNeal and this is Jo Rutherford.' Craig and Jonno stuck out their hands for a brief handshake. 'What can you tell us, guys?' Brady asked.

'The injured youngster is Courtney Pearce,' Craig said. 'Age nineteen. Her little sister, Natalie, is with her. She's pretty upset. Won't leave her side. The other leader seems a sensible kid. We've spoken to her and— Ah.' Craig turned quickly. 'Here she is now.'

'Hi. I'm Amanda.' A tall girl with straight blonde hair joined the circle and linked Brady and Jo with a very direct blue gaze. 'I assume you're the doctors?'

'Yes, we are.' This time it was Jo who made the introductions, then asked, 'Can you tell us how Courtney came to be injured, Amanda?'

'It was all incredibly sudden. There was a rock fall and we all screamed and ran, but then we realised Courtney wasn't with us.' Amanda stopped and pressed her lips together for a second. 'She'd been hit by a chunk off a boulder that fell. It pinned her down. We all pushed together until we got it off her but then she couldn't move her leg. I called the emergency number but there was nothing much we could do except wait for the SES. But we tried to keep Courtney warm—used our coats and shirts to cover her…'

Brady snapped the trauma pack from around his waist. 'You've done well, Amanda, but we need some triage now. Jo and I will look at Courtney first. If you could continue reassuring the rest of the girls, we'll get to them as soon as we can.'

'Fine. Natalie is very shocked. Can you look at her, too, please?'

'Of course we will,' Jo said. 'But Natalie's going to need you as well. So, if you wouldn't mind standing by?'

'Uh, Doc?' Craig drew Brady aside. 'Just so you know—we're on two-way radio contact with Sam and the ambulance base, so is there anything you need?'

'Thanks, mate.' Brady acknowledged with a grim nod. 'We'll let you know. Let's move it,' he said in an undertone to Jo. 'There's more rain building, I think.'

Jo felt unnerved all over again, casting a glance at the ragged grey clouds suspended above them. Determinedly, she steeled herself for what lay ahead. She and Brady had a job to do. And rain or no rain, they had to get Courtney out of there and on her way to hospital.

Together, they crouched beside the injured girl and her sister.

'Hi, Natalie.' Gently, Jo acknowledged the teenager who was clinging tightly to her sister's hand. 'I'm Jo and this is Brady. We're doctors. We're going to look at Courtney now.'

The young girl gave no sign of having heard, her gaze concentrated on her sister.

'Natalie,' Brady came in. 'We need room to work on Courtney. Could you move away, please? Just for a little while.'

'No.' The youngster shook her head, holding more tightly to her sister's hand. 'She needs me. I've been talking to her.'

'Sweetie, you've done amazingly well.' Jo put a gentle hand on the other's shoulder and squeezed. 'But we have to assess Courtney's injuries and give her something for the pain. You want that for her, don't you?'

Natalie swallowed convulsively. 'She's really hurt…'

'Take it easy, Natalie.' Brady began to draw the space blanket carefully away. 'We're here to help your sister.'

Seemingly reassured to some extent, the young girl uncurled slowly to her feet, watched for a moment and then, obviously satisfied Courtney was in safe hands, she turned away and into the waiting arms of Amanda. 'It'll be OK, Nat,' the older girl began murmuring over and over. 'Truly, it will. The doctors are here now.'

'Courtney? Can you tell us where you are?' Brady began a simple test of the young woman's competency. Her answers were strained but she got them out. Locating the penlight from the trauma pack, Brady began flicking it into the injured girl's eyes, relieved to see her pupils were equal and reacting.

'Have pain… Leg…' Courtney's voice was barely above a whisper.

'We know you do, honey,' Jo's voice was gentle. 'We'll

give you something for it shortly.' Jo popped an oxygen mask over the injured girl's face. 'This will help you breathe more easily, Courtney.'

'Pulse, Jo,' Brady directed tersely. 'We need to know what we're dealing with.'

Jo shared his concern. She checked the girl's pulse, finding it strong if a little fast. She knew they'd been dreading a different scenario, that of a rapid, thready pulse, indicating the possibility of internal injuries. She gave Brady her findings, receiving his own curt ones in return.

'Certain compound fracture. Pin and plate job for sure. But her tummy feels soft.'

So no spleen damage, Jo interpreted, and gave Brady quick acknowledgement. They could administer morphine without destabilising Courtney's condition.

Brady prepared the injection while Jo gently made a slit in Courtney's track pants and swabbed the site. 'Ready?' At Jo's nod he shot the painkiller home to the uninjured thigh.

Jo let her breath go. Please, heaven, their young patient would begin to feel some relief soon. But they weren't out of the woods yet. They had to do as much as they reasonably could to stabilise Courtney before the airlift took place. And that meant they had to try to minimise the shock she was experiencing. Jo delved into the trauma pack. 'I'll get a line in, Brady.'

'Thanks. Then we'll splint.'

'Hang in there, honey.' Jo gently stroked a lock of matted dark hair away from Courtney's forehead. 'This is just a little pin-prick to hook you up to some fluids. You'll be on your way to hospital soon.'

'I'll just have a word with the SES.' Brady shot to his

feet and beckoned Craig over. 'How long until the chopper gets here, mate? Do we know?'

'Just heard from Sam,' Craig relayed quickly. 'ETA fifteen minutes.'

'Right, we'll get Courtney ready to move. Where are we sending her?'

'Royal Brisbane. They're on standby. And the parents have been notified as well. They'll make their way to the hospital and wait for the chopper.'

'So we co-ordinate the lift through Sam?'

'I've given him our position, he'll direct the chopper. Walk in the park for those guys. They'll be overhead in no time flat.'

That's all they needed to know. Brady acknowledged the information with a flick of his hand. He knew the drill. He'd done countless retrievals in his time as a rural MO in Canada. Still, in these uncertain weather conditions he'd be glad when Courtney was out of the place and on her way.

Within a few minutes it was all happening.

They could hear the chopper above them, its rotors beating the air as it hovered. Below it, one of the CareFlight team was slowly descending, guiding the basket-like cradle that would receive the stretcher bearing the injured young woman.

'Natalie, there'll be room for you in the CareFlight chopper,' Jo said. 'You'll be able to accompany Courtney.'

'No—I c-can't!' Natalie's face went ashen. 'I can't go up on that rope!'

'Of course you can. You'll wear a special harness. You'll be quite safe.'

Natalie bit her lip. 'I'd like to be with Courtney…'

'And I'm sure she'd like you there as well. And your parents will be waiting at the hospital.'

'What if I throw up?'

'You won't,' Jo affirmed. 'One of the team from the chopper's rescue squad will support you. Just hang on tightly and don't look down.' *Listen to me, the new voice of authority on such matters.*

'All right…' Natalie sent Jo a trapped smile. 'I'll do it— for Courtney.'

'Good for you, sweetheart.' Jo hugged the youngster to her side. 'Your whole family will be so proud of you.'

CHAPTER TEN

'Jo, you awake?'

'Hmm? Yes, sorry. What did you say?'

In the confines of his car, Brady flicked her a brief but all-encompassing glance. Her body language said it all. She was shattered and he guessed it wasn't all due to the ordeal she'd put herself through on that cliff today. Most of it was down to him. He'd totally ruined her day from the outset. 'I said, it's been a heck of a day.'

'Mmm.' To put it mildly. Jo leaned forward to peer through the car's windscreen. It was dark and they were almost home.

'But a good outcome, all things considered.'

Jo blocked a yawn. They'd assessed the rest of the girls at the scene and, apart from their early fright and natural concern for Courtney, they'd checked out fit and were coping remarkably well.

'That young Amanda was pretty impressive.'

'Yes, she was,' Jo agreed. 'It was good a couple of the dads could drive up and collect the girls, though.'

'Even though Amanda insisted she was quite able to drive their minibus home.'

Jo's head turned in query. 'I don't think she needed that extra stress, do you?'

'No. But I sense she would have coped brilliantly.' Brady eased back on his speed as they entered the outskirts of Mt Pryde township. 'Maybe we ought to make enquiries and see if we can recommend her for some kind of award.'

'Someone at the local MP's office should know the procedure. But perhaps all the kids should get a bravery award,' Jo said thoughtfully. 'They were remarkable, so stoic.'

Brady smothered a dry chuckle. 'And not a wimp among them.'

'Oh, ha,' Jo deadpanned, but let her own chuckle bubble out without rancour. She was just glad the retrieval exercise had been carried out successfully. And she could go home to her own bed, knowing that professionally she'd done everything that had been asked of her.

Turning into Jo's street, Brady felt the knot in his gut tighten. In a few moments they'd be outside her house. And there was so much he wanted to say to her. Hell, scratch that idea, McNeal. The lady has made it abundantly clear she wants no part of your pathetic explanations.

Yet when he pulled into Jo's driveway, the pressure to speak of his feelings almost overcame his reticence. He felt his breath falter with the effort of keeping a block on his tongue, thanking heaven he'd left the engine running. He would have cringed with embarrassment if he'd inadvertently given the impression he expected Jo to invite him inside. Nevertheless, there was still an awkward pause that he covered quickly, asking, 'Want to get together with the SES crew and debrief some time?'

'That's probably a good idea.' Jo released her seat belt slowly. Suddenly the atmosphere felt strained and quiet. But not a restful kind of quiet. More the ominous kind. She licked her lips. 'I...should go. Thanks for your support today.'

'No. On the contrary, thanks for yours. You were great with the girls.' Brady's hands tightened on the steering-wheel. Words, all of them wrong, tried to force their way from his lips. Words like *Come home with me. Let me hold you all night. Make everything right between us.* Instead, he cleared his throat awkwardly. 'I'll wait until you're safely inside.'

'I'll be fine. But thanks.' Jo's voice sounded thick and vaguely husky.

'See you tomorrow, then…'

'Yes.'

Brady racked his brain for something—anything—to keep her there long enough for him to say what was in his heart. But he knew that was wishing for the moon. The chemistry between them was way too muddied, leaving them unable to go forward, yet too much had happened to allow them to go back to where they'd been last night.

Fulfilled as lovers. Safe in each other's arms.

Jo swivelled in her seat. 'I'll say goodnight, then.'

Watching her restive little movement as she flicked the car door open, Brady's lower lip twisted in self-mockery. Obviously she couldn't wait to be shot of his company. He lifted a hand off the steering-wheel in a kind of stiff farewell. 'Still friends?' he asked gruffly.

'I think we can manage that.' The reply came off the top of Jo's head but her heart had begun thudding. Today's emotional highs and lows had dissolved much of the animosity she'd been feeling about him. And, yes, she guessed they could remain friends. Maybe even close friends. But lovers again? Not even in her wildest dreams. ''Night, then.' She swung quickly out of the car, slamming the door in some brave little act of finality.

Monday morning.

Jo looked out at the landscape. It was raining lightly, the gentle soaking kind that would have the farmers smiling and the mothers of school children dredging up an endless supply of patience.

She pulled a face, making her way slowly from the bedroom to the shower, her leg muscles protesting all the way. So much for this abseiling lark as a form of exercise, she thought ruefully.

Arriving at the surgery, she went through her usual routine and then took herself off to the staffroom. The partners were all there, along with Vicki. Obviously the news of the girls' misadventure and the subsequent rescue had made it on to the front page of the daily paper.

Grinning broadly, Tom held it up for her to see. 'What's it like to be famous, babe?'

Jo looked over his shoulder at the grainy picture of her and Brady at the scene. She rolled her eyes. 'Oh, my stars...'

'Wouldn't doubt we'll have every radio talk-show host calling us from Brisbane this morning, wanting a comment.' Tom smirked.

'Well, I'm not talking to anyone,' Jo declared, going to the filter machine and pouring herself a coffee.

'Leave it to me, then,' Vicki offered cheerfully. 'I'll deal with them.'

'Just tell them we'll only speak if they make a donation to CareFlight.' Brady offered the gruff comment from his position at the window.

'Hey, terrific idea,' Tom agreed. 'Can you do that, Vic?'

Vicki paused with her hand on the door to send him a

saccharine-sweet smile. 'In case you hadn't noticed, Dr Yardley, PR is my strong point.'

'So, guys…' Angelo's gaze swung questioningly from Brady to Jo, before he bent his head and added a dollop of milk to his coffee. 'How was yesterday for you? In other words, anything we should talk about?'

Brady dragged his thoughts back to the present and his gaze back from where it had focused on Jo. She certainly *looked* better than he felt. Despite being bone weary, he hadn't slept well. And he didn't have to look far to know why. Leaving his stance at the window, he placed his coffee-mug back on the benchtop. 'I've already suggested to Jo we have a debriefing session with the SES team during the week.'

'That sounds good.' Angelo nodded in approval. 'There was a time when the doctors of the Mt Pryde district actually undertook regular training sessions with the SES personnel as a matter of course.'

'So, what happened that we don't do it any more?' Tom asked.

'Not sure really. Probably we all got a bit slack.'

Tom got to his feet and threw the newspaper aside. 'Or a bit busier?'

'That could be part of it,' Angelo said thoughtfully. 'How would you feel about liaising with the team leader at the SES, Brady? Organise our inclusion in some of their regular training sessions.'

Several expressions chased through Brady's eyes before he said levelly, 'I'm happy to do that.'

Jo hitched herself back against the edge of the bench, her mug of coffee clasped against her chest. She hadn't missed Brady's covert scrutiny. In fact, the weight of it had unnerved her terribly. 'I'd be in favour of acquiring more expertise in the various components of their training where we each lack skill.' She forced herself to look at Brady directly, her expression faintly challenging. 'I, for one, need more experience with abseiling techniques.'

'That's very good thinking, Jo.' Angelo tugged thoughtfully at his bottom lip. 'Right, then. Brady, if you'll set it up, we'll get our ideas together and have another chat about how we'll implement things. OK with everyone?'

A murmur of agreement.

Jo eased herself away from her perch and felt her thigh muscles twang. She held back a groan. She'd have to go to the sports centre for a massage after work today. But the rest of the day had to be got through first.

Ignoring her aching muscles, she stepped briskly towards the door. 'I need a quick word to Vicki so I'll catch up with you all later.'

Jo rested her elbows on the counter top at Reception and asked, 'How's my list looking for this afternoon, Vic?'

Vicki touched a few keys on the computer. 'Pretty good, actually, and nothing after three o'clock.'

'Good. Keep it like that would you? Unless it's an absolute emergency, of course.'

Vicki grinned. 'Taking an early mark, are you?'

'I wish! I've a mountain of paperwork to climb as always, but actually I'm expecting a new patient, Georgia Whiting. She's a high-school student. I saw her at the after-hours clinic on Saturday but she needs further consultation. She's going to try to come in after school today.'

'OK…' Vicky looked thoughtful, tapping a finger to

her chin. 'The kids get out at three so she could be here any time after then, I guess.'

That's if she turns up, Jo thought philosophically. But if Georgia chose not to, there was precious little she could do. Except hope the youngster didn't take herself off to some quick-fix practitioner and get thrown a panacea for her problems. 'Just keep an eye out for her, please, Vic. And buzz me the minute she arrives.'

Jo ploughed on through her paperwork, now and again glancing at her watch. When the time passed three-thirty and then three forty-five, she gave a little sigh of resignation. Obviously, Georgia wasn't going to show.

Jo lifted her arms and stretched and then swung up off her chair. Oh, Georgia, why didn't you come and see me? she lamented silently. I could've helped you, if only— She broke off her train of thought, lifting her head to acknowledge the soft tap on her door. 'Yes?'

Vicki slipped in quickly and closed the door. 'Sorry, for the clandestine act,' she apologized, 'but your patient's just arrived. I think you should get out to Reception fast. She looks ready to bolt.'

'Thanks, Vic.' Jo moved swiftly, feeling a huge surge of relief that the youngster had plucked up her courage and come to the surgery. 'I'll take over from here. And I could be a while, OK?'

Vicki understood perfectly. Jo wasn't to be interrupted.

'Glad you could make it.' Jo greeted Georgia with a welcoming smile, and thought the design of school uniforms on the whole did precious little to enhance the self-esteem of adolescent females. Georgia looked gawky and uncomfortable in the maroon pleated skirt and ill-fitting white blouse. 'Come on through.'

'I thought you might have left already.' Georgia sat stiffly on the edge of the chair at right angles to Jo's desk.

'I'm usually here much later than this,' Jo said, seeking eye contact with her young patient. 'I'm glad you came to see me, Georgia.'

'I said I would.' She looked at Jo warily. 'I would've been here earlier but I got kept back for detention.'

Jo lifted a brow. 'Do they still do that?'

'Mr Tobin's a jerk,' Georgia dismissed with a curl of her bottom lip.

OK, so we won't go there, Jo decided. But something was slowly emerging. Georgia's possible antipathy to males in general. 'What about your last school, Georgia? Were you happy there?'

'I don't like school much. Except for English, it's boring. I don't know what I'm doing there most of the time.'

Jo gave a wry smile. 'Possibly so you can achieve and eventually get a good job?'

Georgia huffed disparagingly. 'Work all hours in a supermarket like my mum—not likely.'

'Did you tell her you were coming to see me?'

'Not yet.' Georgia looked down at her hands. 'Maybe later…'

'OK, not to worry. How's the headache today?' Jo asked.

'I don't have it today.'

'That's good, then, isn't it?'

'S'pose,' Georgia agreed reluctantly.

'You mentioned you hadn't been long in Mt Pryde, Georgia. Mind telling me why your family actually moved here?'

'There's only Mum and me,' the girl said after a moment. 'Dad took off months ago. Mum grew up here. She wanted to come back.'

'And you didn't? Was that it?'

Georgia lifted a shoulder negatively.

'Was starting at a new school a bit daunting for you?' As soon as she'd asked the question, Jo knew she'd hit the crux of Georgia's problems.

The girl raised stricken eyes. 'It started off OK.' She stopped and swallowed. 'And then some of the boys started calling me Chubbo...and Georgie Porgy...'

So Georgia had decided to starve herself. Kids could be so darned cruel. Jo blinked, wanting to hug the girl and take away the hurt but, of course, she couldn't be so unprofessional. Instead, she said gently, 'I'm really sorry you had to go through that, Georgia. And thank you for being so honest with me. I know it took a lot of courage. So now I'll be honest with you. Healthwise, you'll be in serious trouble if you don't change your lifestyle. Your body is still developing. You need the right foods to sustain it. Do you imagine a car could run without petrol?'

Georgia frowned. 'I guess not.'

'Well, that's what you're asking your body to do. Presently, you're not giving it the right fuel so it's beginning to close down on you. You have headaches and your periods have stopped.'

The girl began to blink rapidly. 'Am I in big trouble?'

'Not so big we can't find a way out of it. And you've already taken the biggest and bravest step by coming to see me. Does your mum know you're not eating properly?'

'She gets home late. I tell her I've eaten...'

Is the woman blind? Jo blazed silently. Doesn't she see

how thin her daughter has become? But, then, perhaps she was so wrapped in own problems she chose to ignore it. Well, whatever the reason, it was obvious this family needed intervention and skilled counseling, and for that she'd refer them along to Anne Arrowsmith at the Lifeline centre. For the moment, though, Georgia's physical health and wellbeing had to take priority.

'Right, Georgia. Let's get things moving for you. If you're agreeable, I'd like to give you a full medical now. And I'll give you a note to take along to the pathology lab to have a blood test done. That will tell us where your iron levels are.'

Georgia bit her lip. 'Is that important?'

'Yes, it is. So I want you to have that done as soon as you can. It would be very good if your mum could go along with you as well.'

Georgia seemed at last to sense the gravity of her situation. 'She finishes at five today. I'll, um, swing by the supermarket and walk home with her. That way, we can talk about stuff on the way...'

'If it's going to be too difficult for you, I'm happy to speak with your mum,' Jo offered kindly.

The youngster sat up straight. 'No, I'll do it.'

'Good.' Jo sent her a full-blown smile. She sensed a very plucky young woman under all that tough façade. 'Then tomorrow, after school, I'd like you and your mum to come and see me together. We'll have a chat and I'll give you a referral to our dietitian at the hospital.'

Georgia looked doubtful. 'Couldn't I just keep coming to see you?'

'Of course you'll continue to see me,' Jo reassured the girl. 'But Vanessa, the dietitian, has different expertise from mine. But we'll liaise closely so that if you have any concerns you'll be able to have a chat to either of us and get answers.'

Georgia seemed to be thinking. 'So—what will the dietitian want to talk to me about?'

'Mostly, she'll want to have a chat like we've had today,' Jo said. 'What we call taking a history. And when Vanessa has assessed what the best way to go is for you, she'll give you a programme to follow that will build up your energy again and make you feel well but won't make you fat.'

A roll of her eyes indicated Georgia's scepticism.

'You know, Georgia…' Jo swung away to the computer to set up a new file for her patient '…once you're feeling well again, school won't feel such a pain. And just think, if you study hard, you could go after any job you want.'

A beat of silence. And then, softly, Georgia said, 'I'd like to act. Not slick stuff, like on TV, but *real* acting.'

Jo hid her surprise. 'You'd need to learn the actual craft of acting, then.'

'I might be useless at it.'

'Most of us are useless until we're taught how to do things.' Jo added casually, 'Do you imagine I woke up one morning as a doctor, without having done years and years of training?'

'S'pose not.' Wonder of wonders, a tiny dimple flickered in Georgia's cheek. 'Where would I start?'

'There's a Little Theatre group here in town. You could investigate that. Perhaps they run classes and such for beginners.'

'But I couldn't just rock up!' Georgia looked aghast. 'I wouldn't know anyone.'

Jo thought for a moment, conceding it would indeed be

very hard for her young patient to do that. 'Actually, our receptionist, Vicki, is a member of the local theatre group. Why don't I get some details about joining from her and let you know at your next appointment? Sound OK?'

Georgia nodded shyly. 'Thanks. I could turn out to be really good at it, couldn't I?' she added in a burst of youthful optimism.

Jo sent her a conspiratorial wink as she leant across to place the blood-pressure cuff on her young patient's arm and began to pump. 'I'd say there's every chance in the world you could.'

Across town, Brady took his coffee outside onto the back deck. A collection of his mother's books occupied his favourite chair. 'Viv, all right if I move these law tomes?' he yelled.

Vivienne McNeal leaned across the kitchen benchtop and poked her head through the window. 'Just put them on the table, darling. But be careful of my bookmarks, please. I don't want to have to start searching all over again.'

Vivienne bent her attention back to the dishwasher and loaded the last few items of crockery from their evening meal. Then, lifting the pot, she poured her own coffee and took it out on to the deck to join her son.

Brady eased himself further into the depths of the canvas, stretching his legs along the extended wooden arms of the outdoor chair.

He couldn't believe how ineptly he'd handled things with Jo. She should be here with him now, he thought moodily, meeting his mother, being part of his life. Instead…

He took a mouthful of coffee and grimaced. He hated decaf but his mother had insisted. He stared down into the black brew as if it was to blame for his restless mood. But it wasn't just his mood. Frustration about the way he'd left things with Jo was eating at him.

Putting his coffee aside, he pulled himself out of the chair and wandered across to the railings, looking down onto the soft leafy shade plants of the rockery. Hell, he felt like he was in the grip of a permanent hangover. Somehow he had to sort things out with Jo. Somehow…

'Brady,' Vivienne said calmly from her position at the round wooden table, 'why don't you stop prowling and go and see whomever it is you obviously need to see?'

Brady turned and grinned lopsidedly at his mother. 'Know me pretty well, don't you, Viv?'

'Longer than anyone on earth,' she said evenly, remembering as if it were yesterday the Sunday morning her beautiful baby boy had been placed in her arms. Now he was a grown man and with a life far more complicated than she would have wanted for him.

'Actually, there is someone I'd like to see…'

'Go on, then,' Vivienne flapped a hand. 'I'll be fine with AJ.'

'If he wakes up…'

Vivienne sent her son a dry look over the top of the smart rectangular frames of her glasses. 'I'll see to his needs.'

Brady grinned sheepishly. 'I keep forgetting you've been there and done that.'

'Well, it was thirty-five years ago, but it's amazing how the skills have all come back. Now, go on, please, and let me get back to my reading. This is a very complex case.'

'When are you in court?'

'Friday. But I'll need to be back in Brisbane by Wednesday evening. So make the most of your time while you have me to babysit. Now, shoo.'

'Thanks, Mum…' Brady touched her shoulder gently. 'I, uh, don't know how long I'll be.' That would depend on whether or not Jo let him in the door to begin with.

'Take all the time you need.' Vivienne looked up, placing her thumb between the pages to keep her place. 'I get the impression this *someone* is very important to you.'

The edges of Brady's mouth pleated around a resigned kind of smile. 'You've been talking to Thea.'

'Might have.' Vivienne went back to her reading. 'And, Brady?' she called him back, as he'd begun to move away. 'Softly, softly, remember?'

He lifted a hand in acknowledgement. Chance would be a fine thing, he thought grimly as he located his keys and made his way outside to his car. It would all depend on Jo.

CHAPTER ELEVEN

JO DROVE home. The massage and sauna after work had been wonderful but had left her almost too relaxed to move. Her mouth twitched in a wry little moue. What wouldn't she have given for someone at home to fuss over her? Make her dinner, tuck her into bed.

Momentarily, her hands tightened on the steering-wheel. Her contact with Brady today had been professional and minimal. Would it be the same tomorrow? And the day after? And the day after that?

Oh, help. Her eyes filled and she lifted a hand from the wheel to impatiently bat the moisture away. She had to get a grip. Surely shattered hearts mended, didn't they? And hurts lessened with time? She wondered whether it was possible to fast-track the process.

At home, she made cheese on toast and dallied over a tub of strawberry yoghurt for dessert. She'd just switched on the kettle to boil when her doorbell rang. Swinging her gaze to the clock on the microwave, she grimaced. Who on earth would be calling at this hour?

Well, she'd better find out. In a nervous gesture she smoothed her hands down the sides of her cotton trousers and cautiously opened the front door. And froze. 'Brady...'

'I know it's a bit late, Jo…'

'Where's AJ?' she asked sharply, looking beyond him to where his car was parked out front.

'My mother's here for a couple of days,' he explained edgily. 'She's babysitting.'

Jo frowned a bit. 'I thought you said she worked?'

'She does.' He shifted from one foot to the other. 'She's a barrister. Sometimes her cases allow her to work from home. Uh, I wondered…' his head came up sharply and he rammed his hands into his back pockets '…whether we could talk.'

Jo came to reality with a snap. 'Sorry.' She made an apologetic little gesture with her hand. 'I didn't mean to give you the third degree on my doorstep. Come in.' She left him to close the door and made her way back to the kitchen.

Brady closed the door quietly behind him, feeling his heart spin back to its rightful place. Jo's response was more, much more than he'd hoped for. And much more than he deserved, he berated himself mercilessly.

'I was just about to make some tea.' Automatically, Jo reached down mugs from the shelf. 'Would you like one?'

'Sounds good. Mum's decaf coffee after dinner left a bit to be desired.' Brady moved closer.

'What part of the law does she specialise in?' Jo asked, painfully aware of his presence beside her.

'Family law.' He took the mug a bit awkwardly. 'Thanks for this, Jo. I mean—for letting me come in.'

Jo swallowed the sudden lump in her throat. Damn the man. He was getting to her all over again. 'I'm in the courtyard,' she said shortly, and he followed her outside, sitting opposite her. Jo curled her legs back under the chair. No way was she going to risk even the slightest accidental contact with him.

Brady hunched over his mug. 'I've come to apologise for my boorish behaviour yesterday morning. I've hurt you and I'm deeply sorry.'

And so he should be. Jo dragged in a shaky breath. 'I did wonder what I'd done to deserve it,' she responded quietly.

'You didn't deserve it at all.' His mouth hardened into a straight line. 'I hardly understood how it happened myself. But seeing you with the baby, well, it triggered something.'

'Something to do with AJ's mother?' She looked across at him, uncertainty and wariness clouding her eyes.

He nodded. 'Guess so. Indirectly.'

'Oh, lord…' Jo felt a cold river of dread run down her spine. 'I don't look like her, do I?'

'No! No way.' He shook his head vehemently. 'Tanya's dark-haired. AJ gets his colouring from both of us.'

Jo took a steadying breath. She didn't want to know about his Tanya, yet every female part of her was urging her to find out. Perhaps even to ascertain what she was up against. Because, no matter what Brady said, Jo was convinced AJ's mother was still in the picture somewhere, casting her shadow. She grasped her courage with both hands. 'Do you want to tell me about her?'

His jaw worked and it seemed he was weighing up whether or not he could provide the answer she was waiting to hear. After an eternity he said, 'It's all in the past, Jo. There's nothing you could do to change things.'

'I realise that, Brady, but at least I could listen.'

'I don't want to burden you…'

She gave a hard, unhappy laugh. 'I'm burdened now. I don't know why you shut down on me after the magical night we spent together. You left me feeling worthless—'

'I know, I *know*!' His voice had risen and tightened. 'That was the last thing I intended. You knocked my socks off.'

Jo had no idea where their conversation was leading and her stomach was churning. She took refuge in humour. 'I could have sworn you didn't have socks on when you took me to bed.'

He smiled slightly, lifting a hand and scrubbing it over his cheekbones. He felt the knot in his chest begin to unravel. His breath caught on a long sigh as he made his decision. Lifting his head to meet her eyes, he said, 'Top up the tea, then, Dr Rutherford. This could take all night.'

But, of course, it didn't. When it came down to it, Brady told his story briefly and concisely.

'Tanya was the kid sister of Richard Fielding, one of the doctors at the clinic in Winnipeg. He befriended Ben and me, invited us to his home. We were there a lot. Towards the end of our contracted time Tanya arrived to stay with Richard. She'd had a lead part in a film.'

'She's an actress?'

He nodded. 'She was young, pretty, wanting to have fun. Heady with the success of her film role.'

Jo felt sickening black jealousy raise its ugly head. 'So you were in the mood for *fun* as well, I take it?'

'Hell! It wasn't meant to go anywhere,' he said defensively. 'Tanya was off again about her own business after a few weeks.'

Jo ran her finger around the lip of her mug. 'So, when did she tell you she was pregnant?'

'She didn't. I'd moved on to my new job. One day Richard arrived out of the blue. He told me that Tanya was pregnant but that she hadn't wanted me to know. She wanted to have the baby adopted as soon as it was born. Richard thought I had a right to know.'

'Of course you did!' Jo was aghast. 'That's awful, Brady. Were you angry?'

He paused. 'Mostly, I was knocked for six. I mean she was on the Pill. But it seemed she'd had a tummy bug and it had lost effectiveness at a crucial part of her cycle.'

'Well, it happens. And probably more often than people realise,' Jo said quietly. 'So what did you do?'

His mouth drew in. 'Took some leave and went to see Tanya. I wanted to take responsibility for the child and Tanya's own needs in whatever way I could. I asked her to marry me, make a life together with our child. She refused absolutely. Her career was just taking off. They'd even written her pregnancy into the script so she could keep filming. She wanted no part of being a mother. No part of me. She was adamant the child would be better off adopted with a complete set of parents who would nurture it.'

Jo drew a deep breath. It was painful to listen to but the fact that Brady was at last confiding in her gave her a kind of strength. 'That sounds like a lot for her to have dealt with.'

'She was twenty-four at the time. But she's gutsy, a survivor.'

There was a look of almost admiration in his eyes and Jo flinched. 'Obviously, you ended up with AJ, so what happened?'

'I called my mother. She encouraged me to prove paternity, apply to adopt the child and go for sole custody. Tanya was angry. She kept up a tirade, telling me I'd never cope with a baby on my own. And a lot of other things that weren't too complimentary.'

'But you won,' Jo summed up quietly.

'If you could call it winning. But at least shortly after AJ was born Tanya gave her consent for me to gain custody of him. It helped speed matters up. But, still, there was an enormous amount of red tape, as you'd expect. And rightly so. My mother acted as my attorney. She was brilliant. She came over and stayed until the whole business was finalised. Then we brought AJ home to Australia.'

'Oh, Brady…' A great wave of compassion washed over Jo. No wonder he'd seemed hyper-sensitive about his parental role. And vulnerable. 'You really battled for your boy, didn't you?' she said softly.

'And thank God it's over.'

But was it? Jo frowned. 'I still don't understand your reaction on Sunday morning when you found me with AJ. You were almost…hostile.'

He took a careful mouthful of his tea and set the mug back on the table. 'Having a young child to care for has been much harder than I anticipated. I continually hope I'm doing the right thing for my son.'

'But of course you are!'

He gave her a rueful glance. 'You're a mite prejudiced, Jo. You're always so supportive. In there boots and all for your friends, your patients, for what you believe in.'

She gave an embarrassed laugh. 'Thanks—I think. But you still haven't answered my question.'

'No, I'm getting there. When I woke and you were gone, all kinds of thoughts rushed at me. I sprang out of bed and found you on the deck with AJ. Everything seemed so *normal* and you looked radiant. And I wasn't a part of it. I felt *usurped*,' he ended heavily.

'Oh, Brady…' Jo's voice was a thread. 'I would never have done that to you!' She made a little throw-away motion with her hand. 'I just love babies, and your baby in particular. That's why I volunteer for paeds when I can. Oh, God…' she shook her head. 'I can't believe you felt like that.'

'Pretty juvenile, huh?' His voice roughened. 'But inter-mixed with everything I could hear Tanya's warning that I'd never cope. And when you said you'd thought I might need a sleep-in, it caught me on the raw. I jumped to the conclusion that perhaps you thought I wasn't coping all that well either.'

'Oh, you foolish man…' With a little cry Jo leapt from her chair, sped round the table and right onto his lap. And he was waiting for her. His arms came round her, held her and held her. For the longest time.

Finally, Jo stirred. She lifted a hand and touched his cheek. 'What about AJ's Canadian family, Richard in par-ticular? He seems to have wanted the best for his nephew. How does he feel about things?'

'Relieved, I think. That at least AJ is with his natural father. We email from time to time. I'll always be grateful to him. Without Rick's intervention, a beautiful child might have been lost to his blood family for ever.'

'Scary thought.'

'Yes.' Brady tightened his arms around her. 'I don't want to be too hard on Tanya, though. Her parents were divorced. Her upbringing was pretty unstable according to Richard. He was much older, kind of took on the role of guardian—which she didn't always appreciate. Anyway, enough now.' He nuzzled a kiss to Jo's throat. 'Let's talk about us. I feel so bad about hurting you…' Sliding his hand beneath her top, he cupped her breast, lingering over its curved fullness as though driven by the need to reconnect, to feel her body warmth, her femininity. 'I thought I'd lost you…'

His tortured little confession brought a soft denial from Jo's lips. 'Just mislaid me for a while.' She trailed her fingers from his mouth to his throat. 'Can you stay?'

'Better not.' His arms closed even more tightly about her. 'I've left Mum holding the fort. I don't like to impose on her too much.'

'Quite right. Will I get to meet her while she's here?'

'Yes, I want you to. Come to dinner tomorrow night.'

'OK.' Jo dropped her gaze shyly. 'Will she approve of me, do you think?'

'Absolutely.' Brady leaned into her, kissing her softly, tenderly. 'And my dad will love you.'

'It's all happened pretty fast, hasn't it? You and me, I mean. We hardly know anything about each other.'

'You know most of my sorry story.' His mouth turned down in a comical, clown-like smile.

'No, I don't,' Jo dismissed. 'For instance, do you have siblings?'

'No. You?'

'One brother, who works for the Australian diplomatic service in Washington.'

Brady whistled. 'Impressive. Do you see each other much?'

'Not as much as I'd like. Or Mum and Dad either. They run a B&B in North Queensland. That's where I spent my holidays recently. They'll love AJ to bits when they meet him.'

Brady took her face in his hands, gazing deeply into her eyes. 'You're not too daunted by all my baggage, are you, Jo?'

'I think I can manage.'

'And you're happy? About us, I mean. You and me?'

'Oh, yes.' She snuggled closer. *Happy* didn't even begin to describe it.

Two months later

Jo was waiting for Georgia to arrive for her after-school appointment. She'd been seeing the teenager on a regular basis and to date she was pleased with her patient's progress.

And she'd been right in her initial assessment of the girl. Georgia was plucky and determined. She'd taken on board what the dietitian had told her. And the family counselling Jo had arranged had gone well after a few hiccups. Even Georgia's father had been persuaded to attend a couple of the sessions.

Things were moving on nicely for the Whiting family.

And what about her own life? Jo thought, the softest smile on her face as she looked at the solitaire diamond sparkling on her left hand. It had only been a couple of weeks since she and Brady had declared their love to the world and become engaged.

They'd made a fabulous weekend of it. Leaving AJ in the care of his grandparents in Brisbane, she and Brady had flown to Sydney for a reunion with Sophie and Ben. And Fliss, determined not be left out, had flown in late on the Saturday afternoon with her Daniel in tow.

After the initial hugs and kisses, Fliss had grabbed Jo's hand and shrieked, 'You're engaged! When did all this happen?'

'This morning. Brady and I went out and bought a ring.'

'Did you ever buy a ring! My stars! You sly devils! It's

gorgeous!' Fliss-like, she'd wrapped Jo in more hugs and then added in the same breath, 'I saw the most fantastic dress in this month's *Bride* magazine.'

'Steady on! We haven't set a date yet.' Laughingly, Jo had tried to stem her friend's enthusiasm but Fliss had already started planning the wedding, with herself and Sophie as Jo's attendants, of course…

And they still hadn't set a date. Jo rolled her lower lip thoughtfully between her teeth. Well, perhaps it was time to at least pencil in a few possibilities. Reaching out, she pulled the desk calendar towards her.

It was already the end of November. And there was such a lot to think about. They'd need a locum. Perhaps Ralph—

Jo stopped her musing abruptly when Vicki announced that Georgia had arrived for her appointment.

'How are you today?' Jo's gaze was gentle on the now bright-eyed teenager as she slipped into the chair beside Jo's desk.

'Feeling good, thanks.' Georgia obligingly rolled up her sleeve for Jo to take a BP reading.

'That's excellent, Georgia.' Jo made a notation in her file and then looked up with a query. 'So, what's happening with the acting lessons you applied for, then?'

A pause and then Georgia said in a rush, 'I got in.'

'Oh, congratulations!' Jo was delighted for the young-ster. She'd really gone out after what she wanted.

'It's very basic training,' Georgia explained. 'But the Twelfth Night Theatre company is only taking twenty ap-plicants, so I guess I'm pretty lucky.'

'And pretty smart. So, what did the selection entail?' Jo asked interestedly.

'Oh—photographs,' Georgia said airily, 'and we had

to write a letter to boost our chances—like why we wanted to do the course and stuff.'

'And you passed on both counts.' Jo patted her patient's wrist. 'I'm impressed.'

'I did OK,' Georgia said modestly. 'Mum helped me with the letter.'

'So when is the actual course happening?'

'In the December school holidays. I have to go to Brisbane but Dad said I can stay with him. But that'll be cool. I like his girlfriend OK.'

Jo twitched a hand. 'Don't roll your sleeve down yet. We have to take another blood sample today.'

'This is so gross.' Georgia gritted her teeth, watching ghoulishly as Jo pricked a vein and drew out the blood. 'How are my haemoglobin levels now, Dr Rutherford?'

Jo hid a smile. With the ease of youth Georgia had tapped into the medical language quite naturally. 'Getting there. But we'll go on testing you for the next little while until you're right back to where you should be. Are you still managing to tolerate the iron preparation?'

Georgia made a small face. 'I drown it with frozen yoghurt.'

Jo chuckled, placing the labelled blood to one side for collection. 'And you're going all right with your eating plan?'

'Yep. Vanessa gave Mum heaps of recipes. We cook together and freeze stuff on the weekends, 'cos I'm working a few hours a week at the supermarket to help pay for my acting lessons.'

'Well done, you.' Jo's heart was touched beyond belief. Georgia's first tentative step in coming to seek help had resulted in a complete turnaround for her whole family.

While Jo was concluding her consultation with Georgia,

Brady was just beginning one of his own with sixty-six-year-old Ed McCracken, a local farmer. 'I see you're a patient of Dr Rutherford's usually, Mr McCracken. Why the switch?' Brady had speed-read the man's file and now looked up enquiringly.

'Well…I reckon there's just some things a bloke can't talk to a lady doctor about. And it's Ed, Doc, if you wouldn't mind?'

'Fine.' Brady nodded. 'So, what seems to be the problem, Ed?'

The man moved uncomfortably in his chair. 'It's the waterworks. Blocked, like.'

'You can't pee.' Brady cut to the chase. 'How long?'

'Couple of weeks. Pain, too. Thought I'd better come in and see one of the docs.'

One of the *male* docs, Brady substituted silently. But people's misconceptions and prejudices still lingered, no matter how hard medical officers as a whole tried to break down the gender barriers.

'Right, Ed.' Brady jotted a quick notation on his patient's card. 'Let's have a look, shall we? Could you drop your pants, please, and hop up on the couch? I'll be with you in a minute.'

Brady's examination was thorough and he was frowning thoughtfully as said, 'OK. You can get dressed now.'

'Well, Doc, what do you reckon?' Ed finished zipping up his trousers.

'First things first, Ed.' Brady stripped off his gloves and went to wash his hands. 'Our priority has to be getting your urine moving again.'

'What will you do?' Ed sank wearily into his chair. 'Give me tablets or something?'

'No, we can't hang about.' His dark head bent, Brady made a further notation on his patient's card. 'We'll need to drain your bladder. But I can't do the procedure here. I'll tee up one of the small theatres and meet you over at the hospital. You'll be much more comfortable there.'

'Hospital?' Ed's pale blue eyes clouded. 'Will I have to stay in?'

'Wouldn't think so.' Brady threw his pen aside and leaned back in his chair. 'Is someone with you today?'

'The wife, Barb. She's waiting outside.'

'Good. I'd like to get her in here presently and have a chat to you both about what's going on. Your prostate is enlarged, Ed. I'll need to refer you along to a urologist.'

'Crickey!' Ed's workworn hand clenched on the desktop. 'Are you saying I've got cancer, Doc?'

'It's way too soon to be speculating about anything like that,' Brady said. 'But according to what I found during my examination, you need to be checked out further. Can you make a trip to Brisbane fairly soon?'

'I reckon…' Ed looked shocked, as if the bottom had just fallen right out of his world. 'What would the specialist want to do?'

'A few tests, beginning with an ultrasound of your prostate gland, or he may want to do a biopsy or even both. Normally the gland is about the size of a walnut. Yours seems quite enlarged. That's what blocking your water and why you can't pass it freely.'

'I see…' Ed pursed his mouth thoughtfully. 'Makes sense when you explain it like that. So, if I have the ultrasound and the bi-what's-it—will that be it?'

Brady was cautious. 'Depending on what the tests show, the specialist may want to do what's called a PSA, a prostate-specific antigen blood test. That will allow him to make a fairly accurate diagnosis.'

Ed McCracken's head seemed to shrink down into his shoulders and there was an intense silence until he said stoically, 'It's gonna take a few days, then… I got a few cows to milk, animals to see to. I'll have to arrange something…' Raising his head, he sent Brady a beseeching blue look. 'What are my chances, Doc?'

Brady swung out of his chair and crossed to his patient's side, propping himself on the edge of the desk. 'Don't let's jump the gun here, Ed, all right?' he said earnestly. 'This is just necessary groundwork. You've done the right thing in coming to see about your health. Now it's our job to see you get proper care.' Brady glanced at his watch. 'But first we'd better get your wife in here and tell her briefly what's going on.'

CHAPTER TWELVE

OVER the past weeks Jo and Brady had come to an arrangement that suited them both. Jo had decided not to move in properly with him until they were married.

But she still spent several nights a week at his place and most weekends. And she also filled in when Brady was delayed at the surgery, like today, going straight to his house and taking over the baby's care from Thea.

So far it was working well, Jo thought as she finished drying AJ after his bath. 'Let's hope your daddy gets home before you go to sleep, young man,' she cooed, deftly fastening nappy and sleepsuit on the little wriggling body.

Later, she sat on the deck and sipped her glass of wine. She'd made a salad and there were a couple of pepper steaks ready to go under the grill when Brady arrived home. She looked at her watch again. He was late. Involved consult, he'd said.

Well, Jo knew about those. At least when it came to emergencies, they were both aware of the pitfalls of their profession, she thought wryly. And that in turn was probably a very sound basis on which to build a marriage.

At last she heard Brady's car as he ran it into the garage.

Getting up off the deck chair, she went out to meet him. Her breath caught as she looked at him in the soft light from the porch. How she loved him. 'Hi.' They shared a smile.

'Sorry, sweet.' Brady enveloped her in a huge hug. 'Is everything ruined?'

'I don't think you can ruin salad,' she deadpanned, letting her fingertips drift up into the springy softness of his hair. 'But you've missed AJ. He's sound asleep.'

'I knew he would be.' Brady looked rueful. 'He's so busy these days, he's all tuckered out by six o'clock.'

'But he sleeps right through most nights.'

Brady sent her a wicked look. 'So, you're saying we shouldn't complain?'

'We're blessed, Brady,' Jo responded throatily but wondered why, suddenly, she felt so vulnerable.

'So, who was your patient?' she asked later. Brady had showered and they'd eaten and now they were relaxing over their coffee.

'One of yours, actually. Ed McCracken.'

'Has he jumped ship?' Jo's gaze widened in query but she knew it happened from time to time, when patients simply preferred another practitioner's style.

'Nothing like that,' Brady shook his head. 'He had a man's problem.'

'Oh, one of those.' She flicked him a dry look. 'Serious?'

'Don't know yet. Prostate. I've referred him on. I pulled in some favours and got him in to see Keith Elshaw at the Mater next Wednesday.'

'Oh, poor old Ed,' Jo said quietly. 'He and Barbara are the salt of the earth. Been here all their lives. Will you let me know when you get the results of his tests?'

'Of course.' Brady's mouth compressed for a moment.

'Maybe we can afford to be faintly optimistic, though. Ed's not aware of any prostate cancer in his family.'

'That he *knows* of,' Jo pointed out practically. 'In days gone by, few families thought of keeping any health records.'

Brady snorted. 'Bit difficult, when half the time the doctors themselves couldn't diagnose with any certainty. Anyway, enough shop talk.' Standing, he collected their coffee mugs and took them across to the dishwasher. 'What are *we* doing with the rest of our evening, then? Any ideas…?'

Jo's mouth crimped around a coy smile. 'I've, um, brought my nightie…'

'Nightie, hell,' he growled, shooting her a loaded look before closing the door on the dishwasher. 'I'll show you what I think of nighties…'

He stepped towards her and she flew up from her chair and met him halfway. On a throaty curl of laughter, he gathered her in.

'There you are, my lovely.' Jo popped the last spoon of baby cereal into Andrew's mouth. 'What a clever boy!'

'You beat me out of bed again.' Brady came up behind her and squeezed her shoulder. But this time there was no rancour in his statement, only a tone of mild amusement.

Which Jo thought she would be eternally grateful for. They'd come such a long way in their relationship. Reaching back, she let her hand rest on his for a second. 'You know how I love this time of the morning with the baby.' She smiled. 'It's so precious. And *he's* so precious.'

Brady lifted his son out of his highchair. 'I'll settle him with his play things while you have your shower. Then I'll whip up a batch of pancakes and maple syrup for breakfast, OK?'

'Mmm. Lovely. I'll have to dash off early,' Jo said. 'It's the immunization day for toddlers at the town hall. I volunteered a couple of hours this morning to help with the jabs.'

Brady grunted. 'Glutton for punishment, aren't you?'

'Not at all,' she refuted lightly. 'I'll enjoy it. Children are the most magical little beings,' she professed softly, giving AJ a tickle under his chin as she passed.

Halfway through breakfast, Brady said abruptly, 'Let's fix a wedding date.'

'Oh, yes, let's…' Jo suddenly felt emotional, like bawling her eyes out. 'I was thinking the same thing only yesterday.'

'OK, let's nail it down, then.' Brady swung up off his chair and went to the kitchen dresser drawer. He pulled out a large scribble block and flipped a pen out of his shirt pocket.

'You want to do this now?' Jo protested. 'Brady, I've only got ten minutes until I have to leave for work.'

He shrugged. 'That's plenty of time. We don't need to agonise over every little detail, surely?'

Jo sent him a pained look. 'That's what couples usually do.'

'And entirely unnecessarily.' With bold dark lines he began to divide the page into columns. And then, pen poised, he looked expectantly at Jo. 'OK, date, place and venue?'

Jo pulled her wits together. She'd given the questions some constructive thought recently and had her answers ready. 'January, the seventh. That's a Saturday. Brisbane, because it's central for everyone, and in a church preferably.'

'I'm fine with all of that. And my old school chapel has a nice feel about it. Should be easy enough to arrange a booking.'

'Perfect.' Jo smiled. 'Morning or afternoon?'

Brady shrugged. 'I prefer morning. I don't want to be like Ben, mooching around all day, wondering if my bride will turn up.'

Jo rolled her eyes, looking both indulgent and exasperated. 'Luckily, I like mornings too. Then after the ceremony we could have everyone to a lovely lunch somewhere.'

'My folks will want to do that for us.' Brady spun his pen absently. 'They've a huge terrace and garden. If that's all right with you?'

'Sounds wonderful,' Jo agreed. It would take the load off having to arrange things at long distance with her parents, who would have to fly south for the occasion. 'Mum and Dad will want to contribute to the cost, though,' she stipulated.

'Not our problem, Jo. Let our respective parents work that out. Ben and Sophie for our attendants?'

'I can't not ask Fliss as well. She'd be terribly hurt.'

Brady pursed his lips for a second. 'Then I'll need a second attendant.'

'A groomsman,' Jo said helpfully. 'My brother, Luke, will be home on leave…'

Brady's dark brows lifted in a quick query. 'Would he be agreeable, do you think?'

'Oh, yes.' Jo's look was soft. 'He's my little brother. He'd love the role.'

'Good. Looks like we're sorted.' Brady stuck his pen back into his pocket. 'That just leaves arranging a spot of leave. I'll call Ralph today and see if he'll do a locum for us.'

'Hey, hang on a minute.' Jo's voice held laughing disbelief. 'Are we getting a honeymoon?'

'Leave that to me.' Leaning forward, he placed soft,

sweet kisses on her temple, on each cheekbone and on the tiny beauty spot at the side of her mouth. 'Just be sure to pack your bikini, Dr Rutherford. That's all I'm saying.'

Jo couldn't believe the speed at which the arrangements for their wedding began happening.

She now had her dress. She'd travelled to Brisbane last weekend, catching up with Fliss who had guided her relentlessly from department store to wedding boutique until Jo had found exactly what she wanted. The dress was of raw silk, ankle-length and skimming, its style sweet yet sassy and very suitable for a morning, summer wedding.

'You're going to look gorgeous,' Fliss had sighed happily, linking her arm through Jo's, and they'd headed up the mall towards their favourite coffee shop. 'Now, what do you want Soph and me to wear?'

'Well, preferably clothes.' Jo had turned and grinned. 'Honestly, Flissy, I trust your sense of the occasion entirely. And as I've already told Sophie, if you each want to wear something different and individual, feel free.'

'Oh, sweetie, thank you!' Fliss had squeezed Jo's arm. 'I thought you might want us in matching fairy dresses.'

'What, pink tulle and wands?' Jo had deadpanned. 'As if! Just remember, it's going to be a family-style affair with as little formality as we can manage.'

It was shaping up to be a good day. Brady read through the specialist's report on Ed McCracken. 'Excellent,' he murmured. No trace of any malignancy had been found. He should call the McCrackens right away.

He reached towards the phone, then stopped. It would take only two minutes to pop in on Jo and let her know Ed's results. He was halfway out of his chair when his line buzzed from Reception. Brady dropped back in his chair and put the receiver to his ear. 'Yes, Vic?'

'I've a call for you, Brady. Sorry, I don't have a name. She said it was personal.'

'Ah… OK…' he said slowly. Out of the blue he felt the faintest ripple of unease. After several minutes of conversation with his caller he put the phone down. The ripple had now turned into a river and his mind was literally spinning.

For a minute he sat there. Just sat. What did it all mean? To his son's future? To his and Jo's plans? Hell, to his whole life? He drew in a breath so deeply it hurt. Jo. He had to speak to Jo before he did anything. He snapped up the phone again. 'Can I have a word?'

'I think you've time for several,' Jo responded lightly. 'My first appointment is late.' Jo cradled the receiver thoughtfully. He'd sounded odd. Strained, as if he'd had bad news or something. She swung off her chair and rose to her feet just as he opened the door and came in.

His face worked for a second before he spoke. 'Tanya's here.'

'Here?' Jo's stomach lurched sickeningly, grinding as though she was descending in a very fast lift. 'You mean here at the surgery?' She looked at him for enlightenment and saw an expression that looked numb.

Finally he shook his head. 'She's in Brisbane. She's just called me from her hotel. She wants to see AJ.'

'Oh, lord…' Jo pressed her hands to her cheeks. 'How did she find you?'

'Richard.'

'What are you going to do?'

'I don't know. She says she has some rights.'

'How can she?' Jo felt as though her heart was jostling for space inside her chest. 'She's signed them away.'

'She's AJ's mother.'

'Brady, from what you've told me, she delivered him and dumped him!'

'Yes.' He went very still, all his energies reined in. 'That's how it probably looks to you, Jo.'

'Well, how does it look to you, Brady?' she threw back at him. Oh, God, did he want her back? The birth mother of his son? Was that it? Jo felt her skin crawl with dread. 'Has she come to Australia especially to try to see him?'

'No. She's here with a Canadian film company. They're doing something on the Gold Coast, some fantasy thing…'

Jo snorted. 'How apt. Considering *she's* the one living in a fantasy.'

'I said I'll think it over and call her back.' Brady's jaw clamped for a second. 'I think I'll have to let her see him,' he said, almost as if he was discussing the possibility with himself.

'When will you go?' Jo heard her voice as if it had come from somewhere else.

'Tomorrow. I'll square things with Angelo. The sooner I get it over with, the sooner things will return to normal.'

Jo took a shuddery breath. Could they ever be normal again? 'Before you do anything, I think you should call Vivienne. Forearmed, as they say.'

'You think Tanya wants to take me back to court?' His voice held disbelief.

'Maybe she just wants to take *you* back.' Jo gave a tragic little laugh that sounded more like a sob. 'You and AJ both.'

Brady looked shocked. The muscles in his throat jagged

as he swallowed. 'She couldn't possibly want that,' he said at last. 'Could she?'

'Perhaps it's what *you'll* want—when you see her again.' It hurt so much to say it, even to think it, and Jo's heart seemed to hover in space while she waited for his reaction. It wasn't long in coming.

'That doesn't deserve an answer, Jo. In case you've forgotten, I've made a commitment to you.' He looked at her for several long heartbeats and then said quietly, 'I'll let you know about tomorrow. I might have to pass a couple of my patients over to you, if you wouldn't mind? Oh, and by the way, Ed McCracken's tests have come back clear.'

She nodded, biting down on her lips to stop them trembling. 'Ed and Barbara will be greatly relieved.'

'Yes.' He turned and left.

Jo sat frozenly at her desk, her head buried in her hands. She felt her heart was splitting in two. As for what Brady must be going through...

When her phone rang, she reached out groggily and picked it up. 'Yes.'

'Quick meeting at one, please, Jo?' It was Angelo. 'We'll need to sort out a division of Brady's patients for tomorrow.'

'Yes, we'd better, I suppose.' Jo massaged a hand across her forehead as if to clear her thinking processes.

'Tom and I could manage, if you want to go with him for some support.' Angelo kept his tone pitched confidentially low.

Jo's throat tightened unbearably. Brady hadn't asked her to go. Would she even want to, if he had? She had no ready answers. 'I...think he'd rather handle things on his own. But thanks for the offer, Angelo.'

'Yup. It's a messy situation. Right...' The senior partner sounded suddenly uneasy and eager to get off the line. 'See you around one.'

'We'll keep this short,' Angelo said, when they'd assembled. 'I'd just like to say at the outset, Brady, that you have the full support of us all—well, it goes without saying you have Jo's. But Tom's and mine as well. And anything we can do to accommodate you—leave, whatever—please, just ask.'

'Thanks.' Brady gave a stiff little nod of acknowledgement.

Looking at him, the tight set to his mouth and jaw, Jo's heart ached for him. His whole world was tipping on its axis. He must be heartsick, agonising over how, or even *if*, he could right it. Was there something—anything—she could do to help him? She loved him, was in love with him, wanted him, needed him...

But why did love always have to come at a price?

By late afternoon Jo knew what she had to do.

Checking with Vicki that Brady was free, she moved on rubbery legs along the corridor to his consulting room. Knocking, she opened the door a crack and said, 'It's me.'

Brady turned from the window from where he'd been staring out onto the fields of hay that were being baled daily and left in rolls to be carted off to the farmers' barns for storage. 'Jo...' He beckoned her in and then walked back to his desk.

'I wanted to say something to you and give you this before you leave.' Raising her left hand, she slipped off her ring and placed it on the polished surface of his desk. 'I'm releasing you from our engagement.'

For long moments they stood like statues, looking down at the beautiful diamond ring they'd chosen together with such hope in their hearts.

Finally, Brady scrubbed a hand across his eyes, as if he couldn't believe what he was seeing. 'Why the hell are you going to these extremes, Jo?'

'For the baby,' she responded stiffly. 'You and Tanya have a child together, Brady.'

Brady made a dismissive sound in his throat. 'Biologically.'

'Whatever.' Jo swallowed past the lump in her throat. 'When you meet up with Tanya, I want you to feel free of any commitment to me. Who knows?' She gave a bitter laugh. 'You may want to pick up the threads of your relationship. She may have thought things over, want the chance to be a mother to Andrew—'

'Enough!' Brady interrupted, his eyes flint-like. Grasping Jo by the upper arms, he turned her to face him. 'I don't want to hear this. You've been more of a mother to him than—'

'Don't!' Jo shook her head, feeling every pulse in her body drumming. With every beat of her heart she wanted the best for Brady's little boy. A precious baby she might never hold again. But did it have to be this hard to let go? She blinked through a blur of tears. 'Please, don't…'

In one sharp movement Brady dropped his hands and stepped away from her. 'You're wrong about this, Jo,' he said, his tone flat and unemotional.

'Can't you see there's no right or wrong here, Brady?' Jo felt the hard knot of sudden anger in her chest. 'It's what's best for the baby!'

'Don't you think I know that?' His reply was harshly

muted. In a quick, dismissive movement he snapped up the ring and dropped it into his shirt pocket. 'I'm going home now to pack a few things for Andrew and driving to Brisbane tonight. Staying with my parents. I'll be in touch when I can.'

Jo nodded, too close to the edge to speak. Turning, she almost ran from the room.

CHAPTER THIRTEEN

JO DECIDED it was a day she never wanted to live through again.

Fortunately, they were swamped at the surgery so there was very little time to start feeling sorry for herself. But Vicki, with the eye of a hawk, had noticed first thing the absence of Jo's engagement ring. 'Oh, Jo…' she'd said in a sorrowing voice. 'Why?'

'Leave it, Vic,' she'd answered, her voice hanging on by a thread.

Of course, in the blink of an eye Vicki had passed the news on to Tom. He'd come bounding into her office two minutes later. 'What the heck, babe?' he'd demanded. 'Is Brady nuts, or what?'

'It's not Brady,' she'd said quietly. 'It's me. I…released him.'

Tom had sworn indelicately. 'What if he didn't *want* to be released? Have you thought of that?'

She hadn't, not really thought it out properly. But it was too late now.

'Oh, come here, you crazy woman.' Looking helpless, Tom had gathered her in, patting her awkwardly. 'You can't cancel the wedding,' he scolded gently. 'I've bought my outfit.'

That remark had brought a watery smile to Jo's face.

With a final awkward pat Tom had let her go. 'Hang in there, babe.' He'd clicked his tongue in a male kind of encouragement. 'My money's on Brady.'

Whatever that might mean, Jo thought miserably. She'd have to pull herself together. Her first patient was due any minute. But, still, she couldn't resist a glance at her watch, blinking tear-washed eyes to see its face clearly. Her throat burned. Was Brady even at this minute with Tanya?

Deciding their future. One way or the other.

On the way home, Jo shopped for provisions she didn't need, hired a video she knew she'd never watch and then drove home.

She unlocked her front door and went inside, immediately checking to see if there were any phone messages, but there were none. Where was Brady now? Still with Tanya? Maybe they were having an early celebratory dinner. A rediscovery dinner? Oh, lord, she had to stop torturing herself.

She took herself off to the shower. Stepping out, she towelled herself dry, uninterestedly pulling on the clothes nearest to hand, loose cargo pants and vest top. Later she forced down some scrambled eggs while she pretended to watch an evening news bulletin.

The evening wore on. Her nerves were almost shredded when she heard the soft swish of car tyres in her driveway. Her hand went to her heart as she jumped upright. Brady. It had to be Brady.

He was almost to her top step when she opened the door. 'Oh.' She gave a hysterical kind of sob-laugh. 'It *is* you…'

'Hi.' Brady said, his mouth flickering in a weary kind of smile.

Jo bit her lip. She didn't know whether to hug him, chastise him for not calling her or simply ask him inside. She chose the last option and he followed her in, dragging the two top buttons of his shirt undone as he did so. 'Long day,' he said.

Jo looked pained. She was dying slowly here. 'What happened?'

His smile became a grim twist. 'Plenty. Do we have any of that Scotch left?'

'Yes. Come through.' They went into the kitchen and Brady parked himself against the bench of cupboards and waited while Jo, all thumbs, poured out a measure of whisky. She added water as he liked it and handed it to him.

'Thanks. I need this.' He drank it half down and the tight lines around his mouth began to relax.

In a shaky voice Jo asked, 'Where's Andrew?'

'With my parents.' Brady downed the last of his drink. 'We can collect him at the weekend.'

We. He'd said *we.* A whimper rose in her throat. 'You mean…?'

He smiled slightly. 'Yes, Jo. AJ is staying with us.'

'Oh…' Jo thought she might have fallen in a heap if his arms had not gone around her, holding her as if he'd never let her go.

After a long time he pulled back, his eyes crinkling at the corners as he smiled. A real smile that lit his dark eyes and lightened his face. 'Think we could sit down somewhere? I've a lot to tell you.'

They went through to the lounge room. Brady dropped into the comfort of Jo's big old sofa and tugged her down beside him.

'Close enough?' she quipped, wanting to smother him with kisses, but she had a feeling that what he had to say was much too important to cloud with passion. That would have to wait.

'Not quite.' Brady reached out and tucked her firmly in against him. 'Where to start…' he murmured, smudging a kiss across her temple.

'The beginning is usually a good place.' Lifting her chin, she asked bravely, 'H-how was your meeting with Tanya?'

'Awkward at first, but having Andrew there kind of took the weird edge off things. Tanya has no desire to challenge anything through the courts. But she does have some requests.'

Jo felt the tiniest shiver of fear. 'What does she want?'

'She wants AJ to know she's his birth mother but, as I told her, I'd already made up my mind to tell him about her when he's old enough to understand.'

'She shouldn't have needed to question you on that, Brady,' Jo said huffily. 'You're an honourable man.'

'Put yourself in Tanya's place, Jo. She's vulnerable.'

'She put herself there, Brady.'

'Yes.' The pain that crossed his face was profound but fleeting.

Jo chewed her bottom lip, hardly daring to ask, 'Is she regretting giving him up?'

'No.' Brady shook his head. 'She was very clear on that point. She's far from ready to be a parent but she wants to send Andrew presents from time to time. And she'd like photos as he grows up.' He rolled his head towards Jo, a question in his eyes. 'I told her we'd be fine with that.'

'Oh—of course we would!' Jo's generous heart leapt.

But she wanted to give more. 'And when he's older, Tanya will want to meet him, won't she?'

'Yes. She asked for that and I agreed.' Brady's mouth quirked for a second. 'But she wants AJ to know her as "Tanya". She said "Mommy" would make her feel too old.'

'Oh, well…' Jo put a hand to her mouth but couldn't hide the grin that broke out. 'We can manage that, can't we?'

Brady chuckled. 'Shouldn't be too difficult.' Then he sobered. 'But Tanya has matured about a lot of things. She was accepting of *our* relationship. She said a stable home was all she'd ever wanted for the child.'

'And did she relate to him?' Jo finally put the question she'd been afraid to ask.

'She described him as cute, but I think she was quite relieved when her minder from the film studio arrived to collect her. She gave us both a very cursory hug and showed us out.' His chest rose in a long quivering sigh. 'It felt good to be out on the street again, knowing matters between Tanya and I had been settled amicably.'

'It's good all this has happened,' Jo said seriously. 'I mean, it has to be far healthier to have everything out in the open and for Andrew to eventually know about his birth mother and his Canadian heritage, don't you agree?'

'I always intended for that to happen. All I ever wanted was for my son to have a stable upbringing and not end up being torn between two different worlds. And it seems now that Tanya wants the same for him.'

Jo burrowed closer against him. 'So, all's well that ends well.'

'I never really appreciated that expression before.' He

grinned down at her, a carefree, youthfully happy grin. 'I should have asked,' he backtracked. 'What kind of day did you have, sweetheart?'

'Awful, as you'd expect.' She went on to tell him about Vicki's and Tom's reactions.

'Crazy pair.' He gave a low chuckle. 'But they care about us, don't they?'

'Yes. All our practice family cares about us.' Jo stroked a finger around the hollow in his throat, tilting her head to look at him. 'You'll stay, won't you?' she asked softly.

'Need you ask? But first there's something I have to do.' Grasping her around the waist, he levered them up from the couch.

'OK.' Jo gave a nervous laugh. 'We're standing. Now what?'

'Just this.' Fumbling in his shirt pocket, Brady drew out her ring. But before placing it back on her finger he stopped, as if suddenly unsure. Then he began to speak, his entire heart in his gaze. 'I love you, Jo. For your selflessness, your amazing heart, your respect for everything good and true. Will you marry me, love me and Andrew for always?'

Jo swallowed and swallowed again. 'Yes—oh, yes! I love you both to bits... You're my whole life...' She smiled through the sheen of tears that had sprung out of nowhere. On a little sob of joy she said 'Yes' again, and pressed her cheek against his. Then, as if drawn by an invisible thread, they both turned so that their mouths met in the kiss of two people so in love, so hopeful that they had at last found their way.

And never again would they ever have to look back and be afraid. The shadow of the past had lifted.

And Jo knew one day she and Brady would have a child of their own to cherish. But little Andrew James would always be their special child.

The child of their hearts.

1206/03a

MILLS & BOON®

Live the emotion

_MedicaL
romance™

THE SURGEON'S MIRACLE BABY
by Carol Marinelli

Consultant surgeon Daniel Ashwood has come to
Australia to find the woman he loved and lost a year
ago. Unfortunately he is currently Louise Andrews's
patient. Nevertheless, he is determined to see if she
will give their relationship anther try. But Louise has
a surprise for him – a three-month-old surprise!

A CONSULTANT CLAIMS HIS BRIDE
by Maggie Kingsley

Consultant Jonah Washington is Nurse Manager
Nell Sutherland's rock – and her best friend. Let
down by another man, Nell begins to realise how
wonderful Jonah really is. She is shocked by her
changed reaction to him – why had she never
realised before just how irresistible the gorgeous
consultant is?

THE WOMAN HE'S BEEN WAITING FOR
by Jennifer Taylor

Playboy doctor Harry Shaw is rich, successful, and
extremely handsome. Since his arrival at Ferndale
Surgery he has charmed almost everybody – except
GP Grace Kennedy. Grace refuses to be impressed
by Harry's charisma and looks – she has known him
too long! But Grace hasn't counted on her heart
completely over-ruling her head…

On sale 5th January 2007

*Available at WHSmith, Tesco, ASDA, Borders, Eason,
Sainsbury's and most bookshops*

www.millsandboon.co.uk

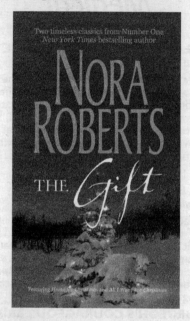
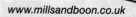

FREE!

4 Books
and a surprise gift!

We would like to take this opportunity to thank you for reading this Mills & Boon® book by offering you the chance to take FOUR more specially selected titles from the Medical Romance™ series absolutely FREE! We're also making this offer to introduce you to the benefits of the Mills & Boon® Reader Service™—

- ★ **FREE home delivery**
- ★ **FREE gifts and competitions**
- ★ **FREE monthly Newsletter**
- ★ **Exclusive Reader Service offers**
- ★ **Books available before they're in the shops**

Accepting these FREE books and gift places you under no obligation to buy, you may cancel at any time, even after receiving your free shipment. Simply complete your details below and return the entire page to the address below. You don't even need a stamp!

YES! Please send me 4 free Medical Romance books and a surprise gift. I understand that unless you hear from me. I will receive 6 superb new titles every month for just £2.80 each, postage and packing free. I am under no obligation to purchase any books and may cancel my subscription at any time. The free books and gift will be mine to keep in any case.

M6ZEF

Ms/Mrs/Miss/Mr ....Initials ....
BLOCK CAPITALS PLEASE
Surname ....
Address...

....

....Postcode ....

Send this whole page to:
UK: FREEPOST CN81, Croydon, CR9 3WZ